ALSO BY LORI TCHEN

Sterling Fierce and the Lost Dragons

Sterling Fierce and the Light Witch

I0609916

ALSO BY [author]

STERLING FIERCE AND THE BATTLE OF THE ELVES

STERLING FIERCE AND THE BATTLE OF THE ELVES

STERLING FIERCE
BOOK THREE

LORI TCHEN

WISE WOLF
BOOKS

WISE WOLF BOOKS
An Imprint of Wolfpack Publishing
wisewolfbooks.com
701 S. Howard Ave. 106-324, Tampa, FL 33609

STERLING FIERCE AND THE BATTLE OF THE ELVES. Text
copyright © 2024 Lori Tchen
All rights reserved.

This is a work of fiction. All of the characters, organizations,
publications, and events portrayed in this novel are either products
of the author's imagination or are used fictitiously.

Cover design by Wise Wolf Books

Paperback ISBN 978-1-957548-90-6
eBook ISBN 978-1-957548-89-0
LCCN 2024934152

For Brenner and Bryce, with all my love.
Go adventure. Be brave.
And realize the magic inside us all.

STERLING FIERCE AND THE BATTLE OF THE ELVES

CHAPTER ONE
RUNNING IN SUNLIGHT

"Come on, Sterling! You're half asleep and look like you rolled out of a barn this morning. You're the slowest hunter in Everen," Evenna the witch teased, but Sterling showed no signs of hurrying along. She rolled her wide, blue eyes and skipped ahead to conjure a dozen blueish-white wisps. With a flick of her fingers, a trio of small birds twirled out of the wisps. As they flew, they morphed into flying bunnies and piglets. Apart from their obvious nonsensical traits, they held a lifelike quality. If Sterling hadn't known better, he'd believe they were snapshots of real creatures from another world.

"Be patient. We'll get there when we get there. And now you're just showing off. Is this the sort of magic your grandfather has been teaching you?" Sterling probed, certain that the young light witch's powers had grown exponentially since his last visit.

Beneath his skin, his witch-hunting magic pulsed faintly, but Sterling quieted it with barely a thought, the discipline hard-won but now second nature. He could finally believe that he didn't have to slay every witch who crossed his path.

Evenna twirled, making her long, silky hair flair out. "This isn't exactly what he teaches me in my lessons, no, but he did say it's healthy to experiment with my skills—to challenge myself. You know him." She swirled her hand in the air, and a marble-size pearl appeared at her fingertips. She smiled, and it responded, glowing white with a hint of rainbows, the way snowfall captured sunlight.

"I'm sure he's just looking out for your best interests—and safety," Sterling lectured in a voice deeper than one might expect from his fifteen-year-old appearance.

He allowed a trickle of blood magic to whirl from a small scar on his forearm, and the crimson liquid formed a tornado the size of a milk bucket, chasing the magical creations in the air. The red twister spooked the winged bunnies and piglets, and they whooshed softly as they diminished into drizzly sparkles.

"No!" she groaned. Her pearl dropped into the mud with a splatter, dimming to a dull purple.

Sterling smiled, proud of his strengthened control. He collected a few more blood droplets in his palm and exhaled, blowing them into the air. An obedient cleanup crew of glossy, cherry-red flies swept any evidence of her creatures into the wind.

"You shouldn't be drawing attention to yourself," he scolded. "Tone down the witch magic in uncontrolled environments. You are not ready to experiment out here. The wrong sort of magic doers could see." He swiveled, scanning the path and nearby trees for any movement.

"Why do you get to use your magic whenever you choose—" she stopped abruptly as a thrashing came from the woods beside them.

Sterling leaped in front of Evenna. His nostrils flared, picking up the scent of woodsy mammal fur. His hunter vision detected tiny, furry muscles twitching amid the bright fall foliage, and he relaxed. Two squirrels emerged, chasing each other through tree branches, quarreling over one behemoth-sized nut and exchanging taunting snorts at one another.

"I pay attention to my surroundings and make responsible choices. That's why," he said sternly, but Evenna had already skipped away. As he turned to follow, he called his blood magic home. He would weaken if the blood stayed outside his body too long.

Leaves twirled in a brisk wind, signaling the start of winter, something the squirrels already knew. Evenna whirled on him as he caught up. "I can't learn if I don't have the freedom to make my own decisions —my own mistakes. Your mystery magic doers were just a couple of squirrels fighting over a nut, Sterling. You need to loosen up."

He wanted to listen to her, but part of him simply could not allow it. She was about the same age as him but far too naive about the wilds of Everen. It wasn't her fault she had been hidden away in a hollow tree instead of learning how to protect herself, but she still needed to understand that she was not ready to make decisions on her own.

"You're right—this time. You got lucky. But a wildcat or predatory hawk could have been hunting the squirrels—and something larger, a bear or feral hog, could have been tracking that. Let's not forget that dangerous animals are more likely to be bewitched. If you tug hard enough, there's always a loose string tied to dark magic. You still have a lot to learn, Evenna." His lecture petered off as he noticed Evenna's shoulders droop in an all-too-familiar fashion. He swallowed hard, remembering the lectures his own father had once given him. He lifted a hand, thinking to comfort her, but he hesitated as he felt a familiar blush rise up his neck.

Evenna's nose wrinkled, and she stomped her ballet-style slipper. "You sound just like him sometimes. C'mon, where's the adventurous hunter I met before—the one who doesn't always take the safest path? I haven't stepped beyond my grandfather's land in months." Then she spun away with a grin. "Race me!"

It's like herding enchanted cats, he thought as he picked up his pace and shook off his morning fatigue. Luckily, even with a terrible night's sleep, his hunter's agility allowed him to catch up to her easily.

"Your grandfather gave strict orders to take you on a morning outing, which I personally did not think was a good idea. I respect him, as I respect all Alins, so here we are. According to the sun, it's still morning, so I have followed his orders. But why hurry? I am sure there'll be plenty of blood beetles." Sterling's jaw cracked as he yawned.

"Don't be silly. I want to help with war preparations as much as the next person, but this outing is not *just* for collecting beetles. I know I shouldn't feel this way, but sometimes I feel like running free—out into the wilds of Everen—and just letting my magic loose. That probably sounds mad."

"No, it doesn't, actually," he replied with a tired smile. "You deserve some freedom after being confined by people who should have cared for you."

Her mouth twitched, and she stared into his eyes. Time seemed to freeze as his gaze flickered to her lips then back up to her eyes. She was unnaturally still for a moment. Then she scowled, breaking the moment.

"I'd rather not think about that, if it's all the same to you," she huffed.

"I'm sorry. I just meant that nobody would blame you for wanting to run free from time to time after what you went through," he said softly as he tore his gaze from her delicate facial features. He'd stared too long again, but he hoped she hadn't noticed. She stomped down the path.

"Autumn is over," she blurted, changing the topic. "I can feel it. The mornings are darker, and the sunlight isn't as warm." They rounded a corner and reached a clearing with bright green grass and a healthy stream, higher than usual from recent rains. A series of splashes caught Sterling's attention, and he scanned the water with heightened awareness.

"What is it?" she whispered excitedly.

He shrugged, seeing no signs of deer or other animals. Then, a glint of silver appeared in the ripples, flowing downstream.

Probably just a school of fish migrating to warmer waters, he thought as he rubbed sleep from his eyes.

"You have a knack for season picking," he said cheerfully. "That's also a hunter trait and comes in handy. Yes, winter will turn any day now. Lucky told me so." He winked.

"Are you still talking to that oversized pecan tree? No wonder the villagers whisper about you," she teased.

"Hey, tending to pecan trees is hard work, and Lucky is my only friend on the farm. He helped count the wood eaters I trapped and complimented my new handmade irrigation poles. He's proud of my hard work. I know my father would be, too, if he were alive to see it."

Evenna's pale blue eyes shifted toward him, and once again, time seemed to still. He opened his mouth, unsure of what to say, but before he could, she threw her arms around him and squeezed.

"You're stronger than you look," he wheezed. "What's that for?"

"Because you needed a hug. And because I don't have to worry about your magic trying to destroy me anymore. I'm happy we are friends."

Sterling grinned and allowed himself to enjoy the fluttering in his chest before she let go.

CHAPTER TWO
A STREAM'S WHISPER

"What's really bothering you?" Evenna asked with a knowing glance. "It's the war, right? My grandfather acts strange when anyone mentions it but won't say much. Please tell me."

Sterling hesitated, but he knew what it felt like when people withheld important information from him. "The rumors about dark elves bringing war faded after some kind of isolated attack on the Pearl Castle. But if I'm being honest, and I know you're asking—"

"I'm asking for the truth," she cut in, nervously braiding her long blue hair into thin strands. She was now hovering several inches above the soil, although she didn't seem to notice. Sterling tried to think of a way to soothe her anxiety as he calmed his blood magic once more. If her emotions were strong enough, she might lose control, and in a witch as powerful as Evenna, that could be disastrous.

A flicker of motion pulled at his attention. "Ah, we've found the blood beetle patch." Evenna smiled warily and crouched to begin plucking the insects from damp patches on the ground. Sterling took a breath and thought carefully about his next words as he knelt next to her. Beside them, the rushing stream bubbled, reminding him of hot tea splashing into a mug.

"I can feel something brewing," Sterling said honestly. "The dark elves have been watching, forming a strategy, sending shadow scouts. The attack on the Pearl Castle was just a test. It's been too quiet since then—the calm before the storm, my father would say."

"You are worried the dark elves will win."

His eyebrows rose. "Your grandfather is our Alin, and village elders are not to be disrespected. I'm asking you to keep this secret—what I've said and am about to tell you."

"Light witches' promise," she readily agreed, eyes sparkling.

"Everen will be a dangerous place when the dark elves return. They will bring an army, and I wish I could help you hone your magic to defend yourself. But there isn't enough time. If things were different, you could train and come with me to fight the dark elves, casting from a safe distance."

He hadn't intended for his personal thoughts to spill out, but her eagerness reminded him of himself. When he'd first learned he was a hunter, he'd chafed at being held back, just as she was now. He didn't want her to become impatient and decide to venture out before she was ready.

"Where do the dark elves even come from? There are no dark elf lands in Everen, but the maps show only sea outside our borders." She leaned in close, eyes wide.

"I suppose there must be lands beyond the maps," Sterling admitted. "They must have ways of traveling over sea, but the shadow soldiers can float, and since they're made of magic, they don't need to return. They're still dangerous, though, and I'm sure the real army will arrive eventually. If they're as powerful as Everen elves..."

"Please train me. I want to fight. What is the point of having magic if I can't use it to help?" She dropped a handful of blood beetles into one of the leather pouches hanging from Sterling's belt. He managed to avoid flinching as her fingertip grazed his stomach.

"Magical beings everywhere are preparing for the worst. Your grandfather has created a way to extract juice from blood beetles without harming them. We can coat our blades and arrows and make explosives with it—it's a strong defense against the dark elves and very powerful when enchanted. Save your magic for training and leave the fighting to the elders and soldiers."

Evenna was silent, then shook her head, braids tumbling over her narrow shoulders.

"He's been so preoccupied lately. I didn't realize his work was so important," she admitted.

Sterling rose, and Evenna followed him along the stream toward a patch of thick mud surrounded by peaceful meadows. The ground rolled gently like a calm sea of grass and clover. He felt lighter after sharing the truth, but when he glanced at her, she was chewing her lip anxiously. He felt a pang of regret. She looked like the scared girl he'd rescued from the witches' hollow.

"Talk to me, Evenna," he said gently, his shadow towering over her, exaggerating his lean, tall figure against her small frame.

"I did overhear something about a shortage of healing crystals," she said, voice quivering.

"War is frightening, and many will be hurt or lost. But it is how history is written for us all. It is part of our past and present. But I hope it doesn't have to be our future—not always." He glanced around and tried to make his voice more cheerful. "Well, we've scared off the rest of the beetles near the water with all our chatter. Did you know the Windly Stream forms the curvy border of Bren? It marks the southernmost territory of our village and is the best fishing spot in the warm season."

Evenna looked around wide-eyed, then grinned and bounced into a flower patch. Sterling sighed in relief. He hoped the blossoms would lift her spirits.

He turned back toward the mud flats, spying a beetle marching along the edge of a puddle.

Hours passed, and the afternoon sun streamed through the trees, intermittently blocked by passing clouds. Their satchels overflowed with tiny, ruby-colored beetles, but just as he was about to call to Evenna, suggesting they go home to eat, he spotted a burgleberry bush. He smiled gratefully and began picking the fruit. The berries had a thick outer peel that had to be cut with a knife. The meat inside was white, but the real prize was the tasty jellylike seeds buried in their centers. The tangy-sweet flavor burst in his mouth after a fierce struggle with the outer husk, and he reached for another. He ate a few more, then spotted another bush with just enough fruit for Evenna. He didn't have any more space in his belt pouch, so he tucked the berries into a fold in his cloak.

"Okay, that's enough," he whispered. He belched, prizing a moment of solitude. Berry juice had made his beard sticky, and he did his best to clean his face with his sleeve.

Then he paused. A faint whispering was coming from the stream. It was only just louder than the gurgling rapids, and it was faintly melodic. His senses prickled, and he recognized strong magic. Berries tumbled to the ground as he sprinted toward the sound.

Evenna stood at the edge of the stream, reaching her hand toward a strange wave.

"No, Evenna!"

But it was too late.

CHAPTER THREE
A DOORWAY HOME

The stream had all but emptied. Its water rose to form a smooth, liquid door. Evenna reached toward the bubbly handle, but she stepped back as two eyes appeared in the door's center.

Sterling ran toward her but stumbled as one of his boots got stuck in the mud. He wrenched at it, but stream water had puddled around his feet and turned to a thick gel, trapping him.

"Let me go," he demanded, pulling on his boots.

"We have been waiting so long. 'Patience,' they told us. We are not good at patience," a voice gurgled.

Sterling flung himself forward, but Evenna was just out of reach. Her eyes were glazed, and her body rigid. Nothing he said would reach through such a powerful enchantment. Sterling averted his eyes—if he looked directly at the water sprite or listened to its song, he could become enchanted too. He stuffed his fingertips into his ears, squeezing his eyes shut. His father's books mentioned that powerful water sprites could control the water inside plants and animals, so the creature might force him to listen, but he had to do something.

The mud has water in it. They could bury me here if they wanted, he realized as he contemplated his next move.

He shook his head, letting his wild, brown curls tumble over his eyes, protecting them from direct eye contact. Anyone looking at him would notice that his eyes had transformed from their ordinary soft gray into an electric glow like an angry storm. Blood magic thundered in his veins, but his blood was not meant to fight elemental magic.

He had to think of something else.

"What do you want with her?" Sterling cupped his hands over his ears, palms facing backward to dampen the noise of the sprite's hypnotic melody.

"Ah, the hunter from Lornia. It was a shame you had to leave the tavern in a rush that night. We didn't get a chance to introduce ourselves properly," the water sprite mused.

We? Sterling wondered. He squinted but only made out one water door.

But then, a second sprite reverse-puddled from the stream bed, smaller than the arched doorway and without a definite shape.

"It's no matter. He is inconsequential to our purpose," it said in a rougher voice than the first sprite's. "We are not here to battle you, hunter," it continued. "We are here to take the white witch home." It formed into a flimsy human shape with beanpole-thin wisps for extremities.

Sterling tried to swallow his rising unease. "You cannot have her. She is under my protection—and our Alin." Sterling tried to make his voice sound deeper, stronger, like his father's had been. "Evenna, step over here."

She didn't move. Sterling drew his enchanted flaming dagger, but he wasn't sure where to attack or if fire would even damage these creatures.

Evenna slowly turned toward Sterling and tilted her head to one side. Then she shifted to face the sprites and the watery door.

"Waters, show me my home," she said meekly.

"As you wish," they sang in unison.

The door shimmered, revealing an image of purple-barked trees with twisted branches. It was not the musty tree hollow of the elder witches but a foreign woodland not found on any Everen map.

"I don't know this place," she sighed, disappointed but sounding like herself again.

"No, but it knows you, Evenna, daughter of Ohann. This is your true home. It is where you belong," the human-shaped sprite explained.

"Don't listen to them! Water sprites are tricksters! They only tell you what you want to hear so you'll enter their waters. Get over here, now!" Sterling shouted. His throat suddenly felt dry and scratchy.

His mouth was parched, and even his fingers looked papery as if the moisture from his body was being pulled out.

"Put down your blade," Evenna replied dreamily.

He clasped his dagger tighter and raised its tip toward the nearest sprite. The door's eyes cut to Sterling's weapon, and a surge of water came at him. Helpless to dodge the brunt of the wave, he contorted his torso to shield the blade as much as he could. The water was relentless, and he watched the flames weaken.

"Why don't you let her choose her path?" the door sprite taunted. Strange music seeped from it and echoed off the water droplets slipping down his face. Despite Sterling's best efforts, the incessant melody of whispers entered his mind, tangling his senses.

"Aaagh," he moaned in frustration.

A sharp pain dug into his forehead like pressure from an invisible needle, clouding his thoughts, but he refused to give up. He strained to hold back his blood magic. It pounded against his veins, ready to become a weapon. Perhaps that would be enough of a distraction. If one sprite were occupied, perhaps he could use his dagger against the other. He squinted through the pounding in his head and tried to shake off the enchanting melody.

Suddenly, Evenna turned to face him again. She didn't look enchanted this time—somehow, she'd regained control.

He held out his hand, stretching toward her. "Let's go," he whispered.

I'm sorry, Sterling. I need to find my true home, she said, the mindspeak startling after the two had avoided using it for so long.

You can't go. You shouldn't be alone out there. You need a protector—you are not ready for this, Sterling demanded.

She gave a calm smile and turned toward the door.

He felt a sinking in the pit of his stomach as if he'd gone underwater without first taking a breath of air. All he could do was shake his head in panicked confusion.

Evenna took a step forward. Sterling surged forward with his remaining strength. He felt like a dry husk. His dagger slipped from his hands. He jerked his feet out of his boots and bolted toward Evenna. Wet, cold mud sloshed against his socks and between his toes.

He grabbed her arm, but her skin slipped through his grip as if he'd tried to embrace a cloud.

"No!" he coughed as he lost his balance. He twisted as he fell and landed hard on his shoulder. Thick mud gripped his body, and he knew he'd failed at his last chance.

"She has made her choice. Foolish hunter—we told you there would be no need for fighting." The door gave a sour chime as Evenna turned its handle.

"Goodbye, Sterling," she whispered. Her skin changed into a perfect shade of periwinkle as she stepped through the doorway. She remained visible for a moment, wavering as if underwater. Then the doorway fell like a tidal wave, crashing against the riverbank.

Evenna was gone.

CHAPTER FOUR
THE MYSTERIOUS PEARL

Sterling gaped as the stream returned to its normal shape as if two magical water beings hadn't just kidnapped Evenna. Grimacing, he flopped onto the bank and gulped water until he felt moisture return to his eyes, mouth, and throat. Slowly, his energy was replenished.

He snatched up his dagger and slammed its flaming tip into the mud, daring it to challenge him.

"What am I doing?" he asked, dropping to his knees. He forced his breath out, along with the snarling anger that had briefly overtaken him.

He wasn't worthy of being Evenna's protector—he had failed in his duty to her and his responsibility as a hunter. He imagined his father lowering his head in shame somewhere in the spirit realm.

I have to fix this, he repeated in his mind.

He retraced the sequence of events, but he wasn't sure what he could have done differently. He squelched across the mud to put on his boots, but his socks still made a ridiculous squashing sound with each step. He glared at the water, willing it to form a whirlpool or whip up another water sprite with which he could make a deal. But there was no trace of magic, only footprints.

His eyes were drawn to a glowing light in the distance. He tucked away his dagger, then crept toward the gleam. It was the pearl that Evenna had conjured on their morning walk.

"Why does she make useless things and waste her power?" he sighed, plucking up the pearl. The mud slid off its slick surface, and he held it up, eying the iridescent shell.

"It's mesmerizing to look at, though," he admitted.

The pearl gleamed as if it enjoyed the compliment. He let it roll toward the center of his open palm and studied it intently. The outer coating was as soft as liquid silk and icy to the touch. Suddenly, it became heavy, the weight of a lead brick.

It was not like the light magic he'd become familiar with, and it wasn't Elvish—certainly not dark magic. He didn't know what kind of magic it was, but something about it reminded him of Evenna. He squeezed it in his fist.

He stood and peered at the burbling river. *Water sprites cannot take living things beneath their waters by force. Their companions must go on their own free will.* He racked his brain trying to remember what else he'd read about water sprites. They were tricky, promising magical gateways and mystical secrets. He should have known the creatures would return after Evenna's brush with them a few months ago. Why hadn't he studied and prepared better? He could have warned Evenna...if he hadn't been distracted by filling his own stomach.

He kept the pearl balled in his fist the entire way home, hoping it would magically tell him Evenna's location, inspire a grand rescue plan, or do some kind of magic. But eventually, he decided it was probably just a whimsical plaything—nothing more. Evenna's childish curiosity was something special, but it kept her from facing the seriousness of her situation. He sighed. He couldn't really blame her—it was his responsibility to protect her as she learned. Dread filled him at the thought of telling the Alin, and he turned to break the news to Uncle Roag first.

As his uncle's cottage came into sight, Sterling found his boots dragging. He wanted to handle the situation like a respectable adult, but the words wouldn't come. He shoved his feelings aside and embraced the sensation of going numb.

Long-neck piper birds stopped pecking at tree berries to stare at him, vying for a handful of seeds or an affectionate stroke from their occasional caretaker. But Sterling passed by, seeming not to notice them. He clenched the pearl, and its icy smoothness sent a frigid jolt through his whole body. He stopped on his uncle's front porch and looked down at it.

Think, Fierce! What does the pearl mean? What does it do?

He rubbed it between his palms rapidly, but no matter how much friction he created, it remained ice cold. He tucked it into his chest pocket and tightly fastened the button over it as he clomped up the steps to thump his fist against Roag's oversized door. The handle was greasy, and the door was littered with an assortment of food stains where his uncle's creature pets wiped their beaks, snouts, and whiskered mouths.

"I like animals, but that's disgusting," he said under his breath, refusing to open the door handle with his bare hand. He eyed the hills to the north and tapped his boot, wondering what would happen if he bolted into the mountains and disappeared for a while.

Just then, the door popped open to the accompaniment of animal snuffles and snorts. Uncle Roag appeared, potbellied and sweaty from tending to his garden all morning. Sterling was relieved to see a friendly face. He searched his uncle's emerald-green eyes to give him the courage to speak the gut-wrenching words. He took a hard swallow as an overwhelming wave of sorrow got stuck in his throat. His knees buckled, and his face went pale.

"What's wrong?" Uncle Roag spouted, the twinkle in his eyes dulling.

Tears welled in Sterling's eyes. "She's gone," he choked out.

Uncle Roag pulled him into a python-tight hug.

"Evenna? Did she run away? Where did she go?!" He scanned the distance.

"Water sprites took her at the stream," Sterling uttered. His stomach heaved.

"How did this happen? Wait, it was the pair from Lornia! We shouldn't have let her go anywhere near wild waters no matter how many moons passed!" Uncle Roag bellowed.

Every animal in the hut went silent, and one stretchy-tailed squirrel fled, scurrying out of a round kitchen window.

"I'm sorry," Sterling said with a big gulp, warm tears dripping down his thickening beard. He felt like a child again, in trouble and scared to face the consequences.

Uncle Roag paced his living room in silence except for the moaning floorboards.

"Uncle, please say something. Holler at me—anything. This is my fault, and I will be the one to tell Tomorak everything."

"This is worse than angering our Alin, Sterling. Evenna is special. It's dangerous for her to be without protection. If the waters take her to—" Uncle Roag huffed around the corner and disappeared into the kitchen.

Sterling shuffled after him. "Can't the Alin help?"

Uncle Roag was leaning out the window, inspecting a metal contraption that resembled a bird-bath. Raindrops made *tink* noises as they were captured from it into a barrel. He turned and seemed startled to find Sterling in his kitchen.

"The Alin left just this mornin' on secret business outside of town—somethin' urgent. He'll return soon. We have to find out everything there is to know about water sprites and where they could've taken her. If anyone can track her, it's you."

Thunder boomed, and purple lightning flashed through the windows.

"I'll go through the journals upstairs—I can see what I can find," Sterling said.

He rushed upstairs to the spare bedroom, the fresh rain on the tin roof barely louder than his pounding thoughts.

CHAPTER FIVE
SLEEPY RESEARCH

Astormy afternoon gave way to an evening filled with the delicate sound of pages turning. Sterling had scanned through every book and journal on his uncle's bookshelves, but none had anything to do with water sprites or portals. He slid a book about dragons back onto the shelf with a sigh. After hours in this stuffy candlelit room, he was nowhere closer to finding Evenna.

He slumped on the floor near the window, then turned to prop the pane open. Rain-scented air wafted inside. He squared his shoulders and took a deep breath, noting the drop in temperature. Winter would arrive any day. The chilly air woke his senses. He watched as the last storm clouds shuffled beyond Bren's borders. The moonlight spilled out, blanketing the village in glistening rainwater.

He rubbed his eyes, as dry as the pages he'd been reading, and thumped downstairs with the reading lantern. He turned the corner, expecting to see Uncle Roag cozy in his favorite chair, engrossed in a stack of magic history books. Surprisingly, the room was empty, but candle smoke still spiraled in the corner, a sign of recent use.

As tired as he was, Sterling refused to sleep until he found something useful. His uncle's library wasn't as expansive as his father's, but it was stuffed to the gills with rare books. Surely, it contained some answers.

"Fairies..." he mumbled, holding back a yawn as he propped open a book with an elegant purple spine. He skimmed the pages, finding only drivel about fairy-dust elixirs and the origins of fairy flutters, or fairy houses. This would put him to sleep as sure as dreamer's dust. He moved to a collection of dusty books splashed in singular but bold colors. The pages of a bright red book were littered with ancient symbols, some Elvish, but others completely foreign. Hand-written passages in modern languages were few and far between, but he scanned its pages until landing on a section dedicated to gnome types.

Fire Gnomes, it read, *are distant relatives of water sprites.*

His eyes widened, and he scanned the page eagerly.

Fire Gnomes are easily agitated, territorial, and distrusting of others—even other gnomes. Born in the Fire Lands, they rarely live in groups past adulthood and

prefer solitude. If trust is gained and then later broken,
the Fire Gnome will mark its enemy of betrayal with a
fireball symbol bearing three distinct points. The marking
is branded deep into the skin and ignites with a painful
burn at the gnome's will.

"Elemental magic is brutal," Sterling commented, recalling similar stories about ice giants, wind spirits, and animals made of rock.

Nothing else in the text mentioned water sprites specifically, but it did go on at length about elemental magic.

"This is curious," he whispered.

Elemental magic was first discovered by the elves. It can
only be ruled by the Elvish race, their one true master.
Only elves may freely benefit from elemental magic, the
light from the Fire Gnomes, the wind gliders' speed, the
earth serpents' tunnels, and the water sprites' portals.

He shook his shoulders to release the sudden tension around his neck.

A light flickered behind him, and he spun to see a shadow in the doorway.

"Either you let your hunter hearing take a nap or you've found something useful in that book," Uncle Roag observed, one bushy eyebrow quirked. He propped his round body against the door frame, his belly bulging under a fluffy forest-green robe, a shade darker than his eyes. Baggy sleep socks draped across the floorboards.

Sterling sighed, noticing how dulled his senses had become. It was unclear if this was due to fatigue or the lingering effects of the water sprite magic, but he was beyond needing rest and hadn't realized his voice must have woken his uncle.

"Nothing too useful yet. I don't know how, but I will bring her back," Sterling said. "Hunter's promise."

"I know, Sterling. But ya don't have to do this on your own. We will find her together."

Sterling gave a hunter's salute, two fingers pointed north, and Uncle Roag nodded in mutual respect.

"Oh, also, your books are outdated. This one says only elves can travel through water sprite portals. But Evenna is a witch, so this can't be right. I watched her go through the portal with my own eyes," Sterling said, snapping the book shut with a small puff of dust.

His uncle grunted a word in ancient hunterspeak. *"Obeau."* It was a harsh word, but Sterling's father had always said it when it was time for sleep.

CHAPTER SIX
FATHER'S LIBRARY

S terling and his uncle rode to Sir Rider Fierce's land as the sun nudged above the horizon, its rays sparkling on the frosty dew. Sterling's thoughts and eyelids were heavy. Whatever sleep he'd gotten was infiltrated by images of creepy, bulging water sprite eyes and elemental magic. He desperately hoped something in his father's books could help.

Soon, they reached the stretch of familiar farmland lined with rows of pecan trees and one modest fishing pond. It had belonged to Sterling since Sir Rider Fierce had died, but he still called it his father's land. Somehow, that felt more right than calling it his own. Sterling hadn't made any changes to the land or the one-bedroom farmhouse—except for one thing. He'd significantly enhanced his father's library, adding extra shelving to hold a surplus of books he'd found wedged between furniture, stacked in piles, and stuffed into drawers. A hint of excitement struck him—he hadn't shown the library renovation to anyone, and Uncle Roag would be the first.

The scent of pecans and rain-soaked bark welcomed him home as the small farmhouse came into view. Its slanted metal roof fit perfectly around the stone chimney his father had built. Though the teal paint was flaking, the aged abode held a humble charm. No matter what changed in Everen or within himself, this farmhouse where he'd grown up always stayed the same.

"It's good to smell father's trees, right Banefield?" Sterling remarked to his horse as he dismounted.

Uncle Roag struggled to climb down from Midnight, the borrowed stallion large enough for an Elvish warrior. He plopped to the ground, favoring his good leg and sinking a few inches into mud.

He grunted as he straightened. "Aye, the rains have been good to the farm. Strong trees and hardy pecans won't make ya rich, but it's an honest living. Your father knew that."

A coppery cat's tail flashed in the morning light as a pair of steel-gray eyes focused on Sterling's hand. He grinned.

"Brought you some breakfast, girl," Sterling said sweetly, tossing a heap of moist cornbread toward Andromeda, his farm cat.

She flicked her whiskers and curled up in a fluffy orange ball, pretending not to be interested. Sterling and Uncle Roag climbed the creaking porch steps, and Sterling whirled. Both the cat and the bread roll had disappeared.

"What's got into her?" Uncle Roag asked. "She seems a bit spooked."

"I think I see what's upset her," Sterling said, crouching in front of the door. "Uncle, look."

"Are those claw marks?" Uncle Roag whispered, running his hands over the deep grooves in the wood.

Sterling's nose flared, detecting critical details about the animal.

"It's a carnivore, and it's hunting. It may still be here," he whispered, giving his uncle a knowing look.

Sterling unsheathed his dagger, and his uncle picked up an ax from a heap of firewood.

The pair stepped softly inside the modest home. Sterling peered around the combination workroom and living room right inside the door. All was still. Roag gestured with his ax at the kitchen doorway, and Sterling nodded before creeping toward the slightly ajar door to the bedroom. He took a deep breath and shoved the door open, knife raised. Again, nothing moved.

He turned to the library and began peering under the comfy chairs and behind the old trunks. Something rattled behind him, and he whirled.

Uncle Roag raised his hands and took a step back. Sterling released a deep breath.

"Whatever came here is gone and won't be coming back," Sterling confirmed, gesturing to the muddy tracks that entered and exited the library.

Uncle Roag's wiry eyebrows arched. "How can you be sure?" he asked, peering at the faint blotches of dirt.

Sterling pointed to one of the shelves, where a conspicuous gap marked a missing book.

"It got what it wanted. It's the story of the Red Wolf. I don't want to think I have favorites, but I cherished that book. It was the one I'd ask Father to read to me when I couldn't sleep. Why would someone take it?" Sterling groaned, rubbing his temples and pacing along the shelves.

"I'm sorry, Sterling, I am. But we have to keep searching for information 'bout water sprites and how to track 'em. We gotta stay focused."

Uncle Roag gave his nephew a sturdy pat on the shoulder that would have knocked over a man with ordinary strength.

"You're right. Focus, Fierce," Sterling repeated, calming his mind. "Focus, fo—that's it! Foes!"

Rushing to the "foes" section of the library, he scanned the darkest book covers.

"*Dark Witches*, no," he muttered.

"*Dark Wizards*, nah.

"*Trolls*, no thanks.

"*Woods Serpents*, *Goblins*, *Dragons*. No. No. And definitely not.

"Ah-ha!" Sterling exclaimed, reaching for a murky purple and black leather-bound book.

"*Monsters, Sprites, and Dark Pixies*. This is it!" he said as he pulled open the cover.

"You know your way around these books better'n anyone. I'm goin' to feed the horses before they start snackin' on the pecans," Uncle Road said. He clomped to the front door, huffing when it didn't open easily. Chunks of wood were missing where the clawed intruder had forced its way in.

Sterling was already focused on the chapter on sprites and didn't look up until Uncle Roag's boots had gone up and down the porch stairs three more times and the man began shuffling around the library.

"You named your shelves?!" Uncle Roag interrupted.

"Mm-hmm. Thanks for feeding the horses. I read about water sprites, but we need to know more about dark magic," Sterling said mechanically, his attention fixed on a new section of text.

"Looky here! *Light Witches and Practical Magic*. This one's sure to have somethin' helpful," Uncle Roag exclaimed. With a loud creak, he collapsed into a chair and began reading aloud as he found interesting facts about light magic.

Sterling interrupted, "According to this, night trolls have long been overlooked, lurking in the shadows of all lands they inhabit. One notable discovery links them to the elves, somehow related to each other, but also enemies? The text isn't very clear. It does point out that troll teeth and bones are often coveted by wizards and witches as amulets, staffs, jewelry, and wand rings—said to be resistant to dark elves' magic."

Uncle Roag chewed on a bark stick as his emerald eyes went dull. "We need to consult the Alin, and we need to tell him everything, especially the dark magic bit," he said with a keen eye on the clouds in the distance. "His messenger birds are returning ahead of the next storm. We best be gettin' to him, and if we hurry, we can meet him just as he arrives. Are you ready?"

"I think so, yes," he replied, relieved that his uncle would be beside him when the Alin's eyes inevitably turned cold at the news.

Sterling closed the book and tucked it back in its usual spot on the shelf. "Uncle, you're an expert on Everen's geography. If the dark elves knew the land as well as you do, where would they attack first?"

"That's easy. The Mirror Sea, where the water is calm and easy to sail in large fleets. That's where they'd bring their dark soldiers first. I'd bet my life on it. Why do you ask?"

"No reason. Except that if I can think like a dark magic doer, maybe that's the key to finding her," Sterling whispered, each word softer than the last as he recalled another lesson his father had taught him— you must think like a predator to catch one.

He didn't know what would become of his mind if he dove into the darker side of magic, but there wasn't any other way.

CHAPTER SEVEN
SEEKER'S SCENT

Sterling's saddle creaked as he finished summarizing what he'd read on water sprites. Uncle Roag nodded thoughtfully but continued gazing ahead from the comfort of his over-sized saddle.

"Am I boring you, Uncle?"

"'Course not. It's just that without bein' Elvish, none of us can travel through a sprite portal even if we could summon one, like you said," he replied, scratching behind Midnight's ear.

"Evenna stepped into the water sprite's portal, and it worked for her, so maybe there's an enchantment or something," Sterling guessed.

"Maybe. I need to think," Uncle Roag mumbled into the tangles of his beard.

"I've got it!" Sterling said. "We could summon a sprite and make a deal for information about where

Evenna was taken. It's a good place to start, and who knows where it'll lead us."

Uncle Roag grunted dismissively, and Sterling frowned, recalling the book's warning that water sprites only made deals that were unfairly to their advantage.

He shifted in the saddle as Banefield began climbing the steep incline that led to the Alin's home. The loose rocks and crooked trees eventually gave way to a damp carpet of meadow grass surrounded by trees except for a sharp drop behind a wall of worn, gray boulders.

Instead of settling in to chomp on the lush greenery, Midnight snorted, and Banefield turned his head and shuffled back a few steps.

"What's the matter, Midnight?" Uncle Roag said, rubbing Midnight's shoulder reassuringly. "You've been here plenty of times—same ol' hill as before."

Midnight snorted and pawed at the moist soil. Banefield's nostrils flared, and his ears flickered nervously.

"Something isn't right," Sterling whispered.

He hopped down to investigate the dew on the grass, rubbing it between his fingers.

"This meadow is freshly traveled." He peered at a muddy patch. "These are the same prints that marked my father's house. The clawed creature has been here too." He stood warily, his hunter's instincts on full alert.

"What could it want from the Alin if it already got your book?" Uncle Roag asked quietly.

"I don't think it was looking for some*thing* so much as some*one*," he replied as he tilted his head and let his scarred hand hover over the creature's tracks.

"It's a solitary hunter," he continued. "It can fly in short spurts but prefers ground travel, where it gains better speed. It picks up scents from miles away, but its vision could be clearer. Its characteristics are like a mix of different predators, not any single land or air dweller—it's familiar but also peculiar. It doesn't make sense."

"Your hunter's instincts...they've advanced." Uncle Roag beamed. "You sound so much like your father. He'd be proud."

Sterling flashed a quick smile but quickly changed focus, scanning their surroundings for any immediate threats. He took Banefield's reins and led him to a tree.

"It's best that you stay here while we look around. I don't want any reason to provoke this thing into grabbing a taste of horse meat," he whispered as he loosely wrapped the reins around a branch. Uncle Roag nodded and did the same for his horse.

Sterling and Uncle Roag crept toward the Alin's cottage on foot, as quiet as a summer breeze. As he'd suspected, claw marks dug into the solid wood door and brass handle. The cuts were deeper than the ones at his father's house. The beast was more desperate this time.

Uncle Roag gently pushed the door open, and Sterling focused his hunter's hearing. The only sound was the tapping of ripped curtains against the wall and papers shuffling across the wooden floors. He inched forward and confirmed that one of the windows had been broken, allowing the breeze inside.

Sterling nodded to confirm that he'd detected no creature lurking inside. The danger was not over—the thing could simply be keeping very still and quiet.

The tracks led straight into Evenna's room—or what used to resemble a bedroom. Shredded bedsheets and curtains were strewn about the tiny space. Slash marks plunged into every wall. Sterling's boots crunched over curled wood pieces and clumps of reddish-brown fur. His nose flared as he finally realized what he'd been sensing.

"It's a seeker—a creature magically formed from different animal parts," Sterling murmured.

"Parts of what animals?" Uncle Roag tugged at the collar of his forest-green robe.

"Whatever its creators decide is most useful. There's a splatter of black residue on this fur. There's only one likely possibility—it was created by the elder witches to hunt down Evenna. It won't rest, eat, or sleep until it finds her. It has her scent, and there's nowhere in Everen it won't go to find her," Sterling said.

Perhaps the seeker had gone to the stream where he and Evenna had been. Her scent would stop at the water, though, and it couldn't follow her after that. For that, at least, he was thankful.

"It doesn't add up. She was supposed to be safe here." Uncle Roag whispered, but his words shook, spitting out in a flurry. "It's too bold a move...too dangerous unless something's changed. Maybe the war—"

But his voice was suddenly drowned out by a flock of ravens. Dozens of them dove from the sky until the cottage roof was concealed by squawking black beaks.

Sterling scrambled back down the hallway just in time to see the Alin appear in the doorway with staff in hand and a solemn look on his weathered face.

"Alin, sir," Sterling began as the wise old man stepped slowly throughout the house, poking his staff at the claw marks and bits of rubble. He swirled his fingers, lighting the few wall candles left intact.

"They have come for her, then," the Alin stated matter-of-factly as he traced the tracks with his staff and eyed Evenna's door.

Sterling nodded.

"The seeker didn't find her. But the water sprites did. They took her into the stream, into an enchanted water door. She has been lost to the waters, and it's all my fault. I failed to protect her."

The Alin's staff boomed against the floor as he shuffled toward his corner chair. His looming shadow passed in front of candlelight, and a flickering fire illuminated a slash mark from one corner of the chair to the other.

"Find her before the seeker does, or I'm afraid the Fierce name will no longer be welcome in this village. This is a great dishonor, and it hollows me to say this." The Alin's words were thick and solemn. He leaned against his staff, and for once, he looked every bit his old age.

Uncle Roag stepped forward and set his hand on Sterling's shoulder.

"Sterling, the burden isn't yours alone. With respect, Tomorak—er, our honored Alin, I'd personally pledge 'ta go anywhere to find your granddaughter. If you can tell us where she might be, we'll do everything in our power to bring her home safe."

The Alin slumped into his ripped chair. For several long minutes, he sat motionless.

Uncle Roag finally blurted, "Hunter's promise, we'll find her. My mapmaking skills are at your service, and my strength potion is working. We will ride together. I can help track Evenna." He patted a sky-blue pouch hanging from his belt that Sterling hadn't noticed before.

"Tell us how to find her, Tomorak, sir," Sterling begged, nodding to his uncle.

Tomorak sighed deeply, but his breath quivered. Finally, a pale white flame flickered from the top of his staff.

"To tell you that, I must first tell you a story," he said, lighting his pipe and puffing a silky ball of gray smoke into the air.

CHAPTER EIGHT
HOW THE PIECES FIT

"Long ago, there were no light or dark elves. The Elvish race was one. Marrying outside of their Elvish race was forbidden. But one elf king fell in love with a light witch. He married her against everyone's protests and warnings. The purists were outraged, and there was an attack on her life. The king's guards saved her, but she was never the same after the near-death incident. By the time anyone suspected that she'd gone dark, she was already pregnant. The child was born healthy, but shadows brewed in his eyes. You see, he was the first of his kind—a mix of Elvish blood and that of a dark witch. He was the first dark elf," the Alin explained.

Sterling thumped into a kitchen chair, wishing he'd taken a seat as his legs buckled. Soulless eyes from each dark witch he'd seen swirled in his thoughts, spurring an overwhelming mix of hatred and dread. He had known his path would cross with dark elves, but their half-witch origins disturbed him to his core. Wherever this story was going, he didn't like it.

As if Uncle Roag sensed his discomfort, he slid a mug of steaming tea down the long wooden table. Sterling gave a thankful nod and sipped the scalding beverage of woodsy herbs until his nerves calmed.

The Alin sipped his own tea, his face crinkling as he sifted through his memories. He continued without looking up, "Eventually, dark elves grew in number. Dark witches helped the new bloodline multiply in droves. The darkness in their blood thickened, and they became unreasonable and violent— different from their peaceful ancestors. After one particularly cruel battle that nearly defeated the elves of the Pearl Castle, the legions of dark elves sailed beyond Everen to build their own kingdom. Over time, they faded to legends and rumors."

"Could they be returning to reclaim the Pearl Castle? Or to kill the other elves and rule in their place? Maybe both," Sterling guessed.

Uncle Roag interrupted, "I came across a dark elf in my travels when I was a young mapmaker explorin' where I had no business explorin'. I'd be dead if I hadn't had my wits and this trusty companion. I nearly forgot about it until you mentioned night trolls last night." He pulled a necklace from beneath his shirt.

"Do you know what this is?" Uncle Roag quizzed him as he appraised the dangling token.

"Yellowed bits cracked from heavy use but harder than rocks. Those are troll teeth, bits of them anyway," Sterling replied as he watched his uncle's eyes sparkle.

Roag's curly beard lifted as he smiled. "You really do have Sir Rider's wit," he admitted. "And you're right, of course."

The Alin glanced at a red, shiny-shelled beetle the size of a coin staggering over the sturdy silver strands of his beard. With a gesture of the Alin's hand, the beetle floated away from the table and landed gently in a dusty cabinet. A pair of glass doors opened at the Alin's command, and the beetle plopped inside a jar obediently.

"Yes, Mapmaker Burdbee. I'd forgotten your encounter with a dark elf outside of Everen. Dangerous business, mapmaking," the Alin said with a grin.

"I had much younger legs then and a bit less weight to carry!" Uncle Roag said as he patted his protruding belly.

Sterling cleared his throat. "Beyond Everen, what is there?"

"Many lands. How many, even I do not know," the Alin replied.

"I've met other mapmakers from lands so distant, they'd never heard 'a Everen. I started to trade maps with one. I can tell ya we're close to some islands but nuthin' as big as Everen. The bigger lands are too far for an ordinary ship. You'd need a sturdy one with plenty o' magic on board equipped to fly if ya run into one 'a those rogue mountain waves. If I were younger, I'd set sail and see them all." Uncle Roag's eyes glistened with childhood dreams.

Sterling tried to hide his astonishment. "Are you saying that Evenna is outside Everen, maybe where the dark elves live? That's where I am to track her?"

The Alin nodded in agreement.

"The water sprites bend to the elves' will, and I believe they were sent by dark elves to collect my granddaughter—to deliver her to them. To know for sure, you'll need to inspect their fortress. You must find her, Sterling. This is your quest—one that cannot end with failure."

Sterling placed his hand over his chest pocket, where Evenna's pearl grew colder like an angry ice marble.

"I understand. But what do the dark elves want with Evenna?" he sputtered.

"I fear the dark elves may be after her power. They could harness it as a weapon in their war," the Alin said in a quavering voice.

"I think I have a plan, but I'm not sure if it'll work," Sterling admitted. He paced along the wooden floor, crossing over a plush rug with beads running in a spiral pattern that made him dizzy whenever he looked at it for more than a few seconds.

He took a deep breath and willed the roiling in his stomach to calm. He felt alone despite his uncle's resilient compassion and support. It was up to him to decide what to do. If he did not find her, he would lose his only home, disgrace the Fierce family name, and his uncle would be forced out of the safety of the village's cocoon too. But worse than that, a numbness crept into his heart each day that Evenna had gone.

He plucked her pearl from his pocket and noticed the lustrous shine had dulled. There was even a small dot that looked like a fresh bruise. He wasn't sure what it meant, but a sense of urgency swept over him.

"I'm going to the underlayers of the Dark Forest to meet with the night trolls. I need to know why their bones and teeth have power against dark elves. Maybe they know how I can get to the dark elves' fortress."

"The night trolls!" The Alin's mouth dropped open, but then his shoulders relaxed, and his expression became thoughtful. "Yes, you may be right," he mused. He turned his piercing gaze back to Sterling. "Be careful in the caves. They are home to many unsavory characters, but the night trolls will not be expecting you. You will have the advantage of surprise. I reckon they have not had a visitor in centuries."

Sterling's heart raced at the thought of entering the trolls' underground caves, and he looked to his uncle for reassurance.

Uncle Roag cleared his throat. "I'll accompany you to the Dark Forest. And we'll have my maps to guide us anywhere we need to go."

Over the next few hours and nearly half a dozen

batches of hot citrus tea, they worked out their plan, route, and supply list.

Sterling stretched his arms over his head and narrowed his eyes at the tiny, round window in the kitchen. The sky darkened earlier than he was used to, but the days always grew shorter as cold weather approached.

"The winter doesn't give us much time in the sun," Sterling yawned.

"It'll be best to begin our journey after some rest, anyhow. C'mon, I know where there's a few extra helpings of meat stew—and possibly the remnants of a black cherry pie made with sourdough crust if my benrawl climbers haven't found it first," Uncle Roag said with a huff, springing to his feet. Sterling could always tell when his uncle missed his creatures. There must've been dozens living in or around his property —mostly strays or unwanted animals he'd found during his travels. Sterling watched him put on his robe in the doorway and motion at the Alin, who was slumped in his chair, eyes closed.

"Best we let him rest. He's had weary travels, and the burden of knowledge and recalling dark times in magical history takes a hefty toll," Uncle Roag whispered. He removed the pipe from the Alin's hand and pressed his plump thumb into its bowl, smothering the fire inside.

The pair watched it smolder, and Uncle Roag motioned for Sterling to follow him out of the room.

"I'll be along," Sterling said in a hushed voice as he leaned close to the Alin.

"Thank you for giving me a second chance, Tomorak. I will find Evenna, and I will bring her home. *We* will bring her home," Sterling said.

The Alin's silvery beard twitched, making his beard trinkets shimmer and jingle, but he didn't look up. Sterling took a deep breath and followed his uncle into the darkening evening.

CHAPTER NINE
THE BEST UNCLE WEST OF
THE PEARL SEA

That night, Sterling tossed uncomfortably in his uncle's cottage guest room. Soft starlight faintly illuminated the small bed, unpainted wooden floorboards and walls, and the fur rug crammed into the room's center. Nestled below a modest gable roof, his quarters were cramped, but that wasn't what bothered him. A dream shifted into a hunter's vision as he drifted in and out of sleep. An image formed—a forest of smooth, white-barked trees with spiraled lines looping around their edges like ripples in a pond. They were covered in star-shaped leaves dusted with lavender over pale cream. Snowy mountains rose in the misty distance.

His body was pulled closer to where shadows flickered around a modest campfire, and his senses tingled with happiness. The warmth from the flames tapped along his fingertips, and a bite of frosty mountain air stung his cheeks, feeling as real as the soft blanket still wrapped around his slumbering body in Uncle Roag's home.

Sterling waited for something to happen, some secret to be revealed or warning imparted. He'd had hunter visions before, and they were usually stranger but more purposeful.

"I know this place. It's in my memories—old ones. But how can I know somewhere I've never been?" Sterling mumbled, but the words caught in his throat as he rolled over in bed, swimming on the brim of the waking world.

Something rolled into his hand, and he clutched it reflexively. The cold pulled him from the vision, and he looked down at Evenna's pearl. It glistened before pulsing a dull shade of purple. Sterling peered at it, but nothing changed, so he set it carefully next to his pillow once more.

When he arrived back in his dreams, his vision was immediately drawn to the hazy image of a girl. She was tied down by shadowy vines, thrashing in discomfort. Then, she screamed out his name.

The following morning, Sterling awoke more confused than tired. He let his toes curl in the bearskin rug as he tried to recall every detail. Evenna's screams and the distinct snow-white tree bark flashed in his mind like scattered bits of a dream. Hunter visions were glimpses into other real places, like spying through a window, but the two places felt very different—the white-barked trees couldn't be the same shadowy place he'd seen Evenna. A pang of guilt drove him to focus on the reality of his circumstances. He thought of his father's pecan farm—and his uncle's creature-filled cottage. Part of him wanted things to return to how they were before he'd met her. Then, Evenna's panicked expression flashed to his mind, and his heart pounded. It was too late. He cared for her and knew he would do whatever he could to bring her home.

The bedroom curtains fluttered in a faint draft, and the sky had grown more orangy-purple than black as the sun approached. Shuffling hoofbeats and a few cheerful farewells signaled that Uncle Roag was finishing the last of his chores before he departed.

"I suppose it's time for another adventure. Night trolls, is it?" Sterling said with a hopeful grin.

Just then, he felt tiny electric pulses in his hand. His grin faded as his fingers curled open, revealing Evenna's pearl in the center of his palm, now featuring several lavender splotches. His perplexed face gazed back at him from the pearl's reflection. He cleared his throat and shoved the pearl into his shirt pocket for safekeeping.

"Best get moving if we're going to reach the Dark Forest before nightfall," he muttered.

Sterling toted his travel bags and food pouches toward the door. He fastened his cape, hunter's belt, and worn leather boots. He hustled outside, where

Uncle Roag was checking the straps of Midnight's saddlebags.

"Good to see you're up early. I said my goodbyes to all my pets, and my, uh, a friend, promised to watch 'em while I'm away," Uncle Roag's voice cracked slightly.

"Uncle, your maps are exquisite—you've done plenty for this quest already. Why don't you stay and keep an eye on things here and finish preparations for winter? I'll be fine on my own. Really," Sterling said, fastening his dagger tightly to his belt.

Uncle Roag tipped a spherical tube of bubbling blue liquid into his mouth without letting a drop spill onto his wild red beard curls. Then, he thumped his chest, stirring a breathy belch.

"And miss a chance to adventure with my favorite nephew? Not a chance. I'm going to stick to you like a hawk fly on a horse's rump," he joked, suddenly reenergized from the mysterious concoction.

Sterling smiled, trying to hide the relief his words brought. He wasn't afraid to go alone, but somehow having his uncle along helped shoulder the guilt he now carried.

"Now, have a look at the map." Uncle Roag unrolled the scroll with care. His lantern illuminated the intricate work as a plump digit hovered over a section of fresh ink markings.

"See them little skulls? They'll sprout purple spots to warn us when we're near night trolls so you'll know where to enter their caves."

"You're not going inside with me?" Sterling interrupted.

"You're the stealth one! They'd hear me huffin' outta breath or joints crackin' a mile away."

A moment of silence passed before the pair bellowed with laughter.

"You have a right to feel some nerves about it," Uncle Roag continued. "Night trolls are vicious, but they can be reasoned with. I just remembered an old warning to not let 'em get in your head—some trolls have a mystical mind-reading ability. Stay focused and don't let 'em talk you into anything."

Sterling nodded, watching his uncle mount his horse. But now he wasn't sure he was ready. He trusted his instincts to guide him in a fight but was unprepared for mind games. With Evenna gone, his mind seemed clouded, and it was harder to focus for long without worrying about her. If he could avoid a fight, he promised himself he would—time was not on his side. Besides, enemies of his enemy couldn't be that bad, right?

Uncle Roag gripped his nephew's forearm, leaning in from Midnight's oversized saddle.

"Your blood magic is strong. There isn't a witch or enemy you cannot defeat if you're smart about it." He straightened in the saddle and began chanting an old hunter's tune that Sir Rider used to hum before big hunts.

Sterling mounted Banefield and stroked the horse's silky, silver coat for good luck.

"I'm proud to travel alongside you, Roag Burdbee, master mapmaker, and the best uncle west o' the Pearl Sea," he said, and they spurred their horses toward the westward path out of Bren.

CHAPTER TEN
A HOLE IN THE GROUND

The travelers continued humming old hunter's tunes as the sun climbed higher over wavy wheat fields, shimmering on the season's last golden foliage. They followed the well-defined dirt path that stretched beyond Bren, rounding squatty trees and clumps of wild frost bushes. The frost berries would flourish as most other living things tucked in for the winter. Sterling enjoyed the warmth of sunlight on his back, balancing the cool notes in the wind. It allowed him to relax long enough to formulate pieces of a plan for when he encountered the night trolls.

Eventually, they turned to follow the Great River, and it was midday when they passed the outskirts of Lornia. Its great stone walls stood as imposing as always. After a brief rest for their horses, they rode on, crossing the Great Bridge, sturdy from fresh repairs. Birds swooped through the evening breeze, but as the shadows of the Dark Forest loomed, even this faint fluttering became scarce. The chest-deep grass had developed dried brown edges as if even rain had avoided this place.

"Here's the entrance." Sterling lifted a spiky branch to reveal an overgrown trail. He let Uncle Roag through, then let the branch drop behind Banefield. Inside, there was only darkness, except for splotches of pale green tree sap—beautiful despite its odor of stale sweetness. Occasionally, shelled tree fruit clunked together from a rogue wind current or moth wings fluttered with a *piff-piff-piff* sound as the bug fled an encounter with the forest's unexpected guests.

The hair on Sterling's arms rose, but his hunter instincts had sharpened notably since the last time he'd been here, and he led the way, unworried but alert. He scanned the trees toward Mirror Lake, where he'd met a dark witch for the first time. Understandably, his pulse thumped feverishly against his forearms. Sterling felt a sense of dread, but not about dark witches—it was the hollowness of self-doubt. Had he learned enough to handle night trolls or dark elves? Even if he could win in combat, he couldn't be sure his instincts were strong enough to track Evenna.

"Don't look so serious. You're starting to make me nervous." Uncle Roag drew his horse close, signaling toward the glow-in-the-dark bugs blinking on and off. "Look, most things follow the flow of the natural world around 'em, and it's enough to get by. Sometimes, you just have to trust yourself."

Sterling forced a smile and admired the glow bugs.

Thickets of trees soared above his head and carpets of mushrooms popped up through decayed logs. He cringed as they passed beneath twisted tree branches forming an unruly arch he did not recognize. It was enough to tell any sensible traveler to turn around. Banefield tugged his head in the opposite direction.

"I know you don't like it here. Neither do I, but we have to do this—it's one step closer to getting Evenna back," Sterling whispered.

Banefield snorted.

It had been a full day of riding, but his uncle appeared as sprightly as ever, thanks to his special blue "healthy juice." However, Sterling felt a tinge of fatigue, and by the strong aroma of horse sweat permeating the air, the horses needed a break. They started to look for a safe place to stop, but the path was deceptive, and they had to retrace their steps several times to get back on the true path. The horses slowed to a shuffling pace as the darkness intensified. Any glimmer of sap residue was gone. Sterling uncorked a small glass bottle and scooped in a flying glow beetle from the air.

"That'll do nicely," he said, dropping a sugar cube into the bottle before recorking it. He tapped the glass, and a yellow light popped on, enough to illuminate the path a few steps ahead.

"Ah yes, the hunters' lantern," Uncle Roag said as he trapped a pair of whisper moths in an empty lantern. The moths' wings sparked purple-and-white light as they fluttered in the glass.

"I need to check something," Sterling said as he unrolled the map, stretching the paper toward the lantern. He strained to make out the words *The Caves*.

"Here," he directed, pointing to a large section of the map. There was a droplet on the map, unusual in his uncle's prized work. He chuckled, imagining his uncle steadying an ink pen, slippery from perspiration, and his monocle wedged over one eye, clouded from hot breath.

"What's got into you?" Uncle Roag hissed.

"I was just remembering your monocle."

"My 'ghost eye'! I'd chase you 'round the farm pretendin' to be a spirit. Your father never approved of that game," Uncle Roag chuckled.

Just then, Banefield balked.

"Banefield, what's wrong?!" Sterling demanded, but it wasn't hard to figure out.

A wide hole had been torn across the dirt path, as if an enormous beast had scraped it with a single claw. It was relatively fresh, as no vegetation had grown along the walls.

"It was dug some time ago," Sterling concluded, noting the trickles of erosion along the sides.

"But why was it dug in the first place?" Uncle Roag asked. "No one travels these woods except for the lone daredevil or lost soul."

"It's strange," Sterling commented, already having slid out of his saddle. He led Banefield by the reins, stepping around the churned earth and thrashing through the tall grass.

"If I didn't know better, it looks like the kind o' hole to bury the dead," Uncle Roag whispered.

A chill shot up his spine, the kind of primal warning he presumed his horse felt with each step deeper into these woods.

"The Dark Forest isn't guarded by any race. It allows magical creatures and feral animals to live in the shadows. Anything could be out here," Sterling confirmed.

"Best we take a look. I don't want any more surprises," Uncle Roag said in a hushed voice as he loosened his bow and arrow from his pack. He positioned a squatty arrow against the bowstring and took aim into the hole.

Sterling drew his blade and crept forward, senses on high alert. He lifted his lantern over the edge and peered at the bottom.

"Dead blood beetles," he announced.

Uncle Roag crouched and used his bow to scoop up a few beetles and examine them. Each was mature, large enough to fill his palm, and coated in a dark purple residue.

"A thousand or more," Sterling gulped.

"The dark elves are behind this," Uncle Roag confirmed. "They know we need 'em for the war. Anyone collecting blood beetles needs to be warned."

Sterling wanted to ride as fast as Banefield could carry him, village by village, to make sure everyone knew the ghost soldiers were hunting areas where blood beetles burrowed. Most who collected them were not warriors, but innocent farmers and children wanting to help protect their homes. He grunted, punching a moss-covered tree as his blood warmed, rippling across his skin's surface.

"But right now, we have to stay focused on Evenna no matter what," his uncle's words stung.

"Evenna," Sterling repeated her name, and his blood magic stood down. He retreated to his horse and took a deep breath.

"We go on foot from here. We can't risk injuring the horses in a pit, in case there are more like this one," he explained.

Leading their mounts, they traipsed through a dizzying maze of trees in night troll territory. A few more wrong turns later, finally, their efforts paid off as a clearing of widely spaced trees appeared. A musky scent oozed from the earth as they crept over mashed grass and mushrooms torn from being stepped on by something very heavy.

"We're probably standing over a network of caves right now," Sterling noted. "Is this mossy boulder sufficient?"

"It'll keep me and the horses hidden for now."

Something snapped in the distance, and Uncle Roag peered at the shadowy foliage.

"Best be finding the entrance," he whispered.

Sterling listened to the forest. He needed time to solidify a plan once inside the caves. Vibrations pulsed from underground, and he followed them. He slipped through the spaces between trees, calculating possible plans. Another rumble vibrated underfoot. Sterling clutched his dagger and pressed himself against a huge fallen tree. The former giant of the forest was as wide as his house and probably a thousand years old, although it had certainly been lying on its side for years, for moss and mushrooms sprouting along its length. The vibrations seemed stronger here. Sterling analyzed the curves of the bark until his gaze came to rest on a curved outline where no fungi grew. He squinted and slowly leaned forward. But his boot slipped on a patch of leaves, heaving his body against a wooden knot the size of a dinner plate. Tree bark rumbled as the curved outline rotated downward, revealing a pitch-black hole and releasing a sour stench. Sterling leaned back, falling on his butt to avoid sliding into the darkness.

"A hole in the ground can always be found beneath Everen's decay. A place out of sight, a troll's delight, to dwell in the day before hunting at night. Best stay away or get a troll's bite. Then never again will you see the sun's light," Sterling whispered the words of a children's song. He was discovering that many such rhymes had more truth than he had guessed when he was young.

He took a deep breath and said a hunter's prayer before releasing his grip on the doorway. Down the musty black hole, he braced for whatever would break his fall.

CHAPTER ELEVEN

GREEN BLOOD

S terling landed on all fours at the bottom of the troll tunnel. The air reeked like rotten cheese, magnified as the entrance door rolled shut. The space was empty and dark, the only light a faint crease around the entrance—much higher than he'd realized. If he had to leave the same way he'd come in, it was well beyond his jumping ability. But he'd have to worry about that later.

He scanned the slope of the cave, committing it to memory. His night vision slowly activated, revealing more details. Tree roots had squirmed through the rounded walls, but something twice as tall as Sterling had punched through the dangling appendages to create a gap. Sterling scrambled over a mess of muddy roots and found himself at a dead end.

"It's not an end. It's a beginning. Another hidden door," he whispered, running his fingers along the gnarled root ball affixed to one side. It was adorned with skull fragments. He shoved it with all his weight, and a nearby stone slab jiggled. Sterling rolled it just far enough to squeeze through before it thudded back into place. He was now in a smooth tunnel that extended straight as far as he could see.

If he hadn't been holding his breath from the foul odor, he'd have yelped when something tickled the back of his leg. He slowly turned to inspect the damp wall behind him. An assortment of glistening beetles, dweller ants, and plump, two-headed worms harnessing hooked, digging claws crawled freely over the walls. Some wriggled over his boots and up his pant leg. None seemed to mind the human intruder as they scurried around their underground haven.

He tried his best to block out the thousands of tiny insect legs tapping. The bugs weren't a concern, but when a winged slug fell from above and suctioned onto Sterling's forehead, he grew irritated with the underground crowd. Slugs were a source of disease— even touching them could be near fatal, depending on the species. He shook his head strategically, sprinting forward with his head tilted down to help the slug slide down his cheek. Finally, it plopped onto the ground.

"There you go, big guy. Go about your way," he smiled, wiping the snot-like goo off his forehead with his cape.

The tunnel seemed to go on forever, and Sterling sped up. He was soon jogging at a steady pace, his footfalls light and his hood raised to prevent more tiny hitchhikers. Something pressed into his chest, and suddenly, Sterling was slung backward. His body wobbled, held in place by something elastic. He was entangled in a sticky, iridescent mesh. He snatched it away from his face, but it clung to his fingers. And it vibrated. Something was coming. Sterling used his free hand to unsheathe his dagger as he peered into the gloom, tugging desperately to disentangle his feet, which bounced just out of reach of the reassuring cave floor. A tiny insect scrambled across the inside of his shirt, up and down his back, searching for a way out. It tickled painfully, but he dared not lose focus.

A dark mass was hurtling along the cave ceiling. And then it was upon him. He caught a glimpse of beady black eyes and a long, thorny body the size of a full-grown hog. Prickly legs snatched at Sterling, wrapping more of the mesh around him.

Hunter blood, what a tasty delight. The creature's voice seemed to whisper from all around.

Sterling slashed at the webbing, freeing his arms and legs, but each time he cut away a section, the creature was upon him, stabbing and rewrapping. He slashed at the insect legs, but the beast was too fast. No matter how many times he tried, the multiplying legs had the advantage. In raw frustration, he spit in the creature's eyes. It hissed, curling one greasy leg tightly around Sterling's stomach and drenching his shirt in cold goo.

While it was distracted, he aimed his dagger again, but another one of its many legs whipped around, striking his face. The blade bit through a section of web, and Sterling dropped, but the creature caught him before he hit the ground. Another whiplike leg knocked his blade from his hand. It clanged as it bounced against the rock wall and landed just out of reach. But it didn't matter. Even if he could fetch it, the cave bug had an army of legs at its disposal and motion-sensitive eyes designed for the darkness. Worse than that, his attacker's midsection sloshed with digestion liquids inside an empty cavity. It was starving, and there were few forces in the wild more dangerous than hunger.

A chilling squeal came out of the creature as its scissor-like pincer slashed Sterling's face. The wound burned intensely, then grew numb. His hunter's sight began to dim. Soon he would be in total darkness. He bucked and kicked the giant thorned creature with all his might.

Yes, squirm and resist, young hunter! It makes eating you whole much more enticing—a wiggling meal tickles on the way down!

Two more legs appeared, pulling on Sterling's arms, and they tossed him against the muddy ceiling. He stuck to it somehow, and the cave floor spun into unrecognizable shadows.

When he opened his eyes, somehow the dizziness was gone and his hunter's vision was back, though hazy. His body was immobile, cocooned in silky webbing. He was pressed against the ceiling, and the giant bug was lowering what looked like a giant iridescent sock over his head.

Without an actual witch to fight, he'd learned that thinking of one mustered similar energy in his body and could summon his blood magic. It didn't always work, but right now, he needed it to. He concentrated on the idea of a dark witch cackling over the idea of eating him. His blood magic stirred sluggishly beneath his veins, then began to pulse.

"You'll be sorry you tried to eat me, you oversized house pest!" Sterling warned.

Glossy red ropes shot out from his forearms, piercing through the tight webbing. His blood magic wrapped around the creature's hind legs and squeezed until there was a sickening crunch. The beast shrieked, striking a needlelike leg at Sterling's neck. The blood reformed into a shield, saving him from a punctured eye. The leg skidded off, and his blood reformed into a sturdy sword. Threads of green trickled through it, and Sterling frowned at it.

That was all the opening the creature needed. Its thorned head was suddenly in his face, fangs piercing his scalp. Ironically, the webbing sock prevented the creature from biting clean through his skin, and the jolt of pain spurred Sterling into action. The scarlet sword slammed through the creature's head, and its jaws grew slack. The thing clattered to the ground, and Sterling used his flickering sword to cut away the threads that secured him to the ceiling.

The rubbery webbing that still clung to his body

took most of the impact of the fall, allowing Sterling to gently bounce to a stop.

The beast's myriad eyes were dull and still, reflecting a sweaty human face with a ragged fang wound cutting across it. Sterling summoned a small blood ax to cut away the webs around his arm. He stared at it as it worked. Sickly green insect venom swirled in the crimson blade, and each time it trickled to the edge, the ax collapsed and had to reform. His blood magic may be keeping the venom from reaching his heart, but the poison wasn't harmless. He allowed the faltering ax to withdraw into his body and searched for his dagger to finish clearing the webbing from his body.

"Good work. We need to recharge—there are worse things down here," he whispered to his blood.

The sound of distant thumping made his stomach churn. He had to move on. Cave bugs lived in large numbers, and when the family smelled blood of their own, they would hunt him down.

Down a massive passageway, he ran with hunter speed. It led to a solitary landing that dropped off to a steep decline. With the rumbling vibrations of creatures moving about the cave ringing in his ears, he slid down, half rolling, half falling, before crashing into a stone statue at the bottom. It wore a crown of skulls and a necklace of pointed quills that hung down to a bulbous belly. Painted symbols covered his face, arms, and stomach. Though Sterling couldn't read any of them, he knew this was an image of the

Night Troll King. Bristly hair covered its shoulders and groin. A set of fanged teeth rested outside his mouth, just like the cave bug's pinchers.

He shuddered as his heartbeat slowed after his desperate run. Each cut, bang, and bruise announced themselves with varying types of pain. Sterling brushed the dust from his knees and tried to ignore the throbbing in his cheek, the worst of his injuries. The pain had spread to his jaw, but so far, his blood magic had been able to keep the toxins at bay, yet at what cost?

Moving past the statue brought him to a maze of stone hallways. Seven separate paths reared up before him with no indication where they would lead. He shut his eyes and listened intently. He listened for the stomping of a solitary night troll, but instead, the sound of insect legs pounded in the distance, hunting him. Sweat beaded on his neck, and he forced his mind to concentrate. Finally, the faint sound of heavy, distant footsteps echoed from one of the halls. Crunching, chewing, and breathing noises whirled into his ears from three more hallways, blurring them into a chaotic chorus of confusion.

He lifted his hand to his chest, brushing the pocket where Evenna's pearl was secured. A wave of calmness washed over him.

"Evenna, please help me find the night trolls?" he asked the tiny magical ball. If he'd been hoping for her to mindspeak back to him, he was disappointed. Yet perhaps she had heard him.

What happened next could have been the result of hunter's luck, witch magic, or simply being in the right place at the right time. All went quiet except for the breathing of one solitary, heavy set of lungs. He drew his dagger and disappeared down hall number six as a pack of thorned cave creatures flooded the stone landing.

CHAPTER TWELVE

THE TROLL'S CURSE

Sterling ran hard enough that the slash on his face began to throb as his pulse raced. The tunnel was wide enough for three or four horses to pass side by side, and he felt better putting as much distance as possible between him and the cave crawlers. The curved tunnel walls were now entirely of stone, which hopefully wouldn't leave much of a trace for cave bugs to track. Unfortunately, the bloody wound on his head was oozing, and the trickling droplets of blood and toxins burned as they slid down his cheek and pattered to the floor. He willed his blood magic to control the poison, but as he did so, his night vision dimmed. He was quickly losing his advantages, and with a trail of blood leading right to him, he didn't like his chances. *Maybe they will go down the wrong tunnels*, he hoped. He took in a ragged breath and tried to put on a burst of speed.

He refused to look back. The damp, dark underground reminded him of witches, but even they didn't smell as bad as these caves. The cold numbed the gash across his face, and the pain was bearable for now. That, or the toxins numbed his facial tissue. Either way, he wouldn't let it slow him down, not even as the temperature dropped below freezing.

After reaching what appeared to be a dead end, he stopped to catch his breath. A pounding headache began, and thick stone walls felt like they were closing in on him. He snatched his water flask and thrust the spout to his lips. Two drops trickled out. The horn container must have leaked during his fight. He hurled the flask in frustration. It clattered against the wall, and he immediately regretted making so much noise. He tried to summon his blood magic, but all he could manage was a small dagger twisted with green tendrils. He tried to guide the toxins out of his body, but his sword hand immediately grew numb, and he hurried to isolate the poison once more. He couldn't allow his strength to be impaired along with his control and magic.

"I've got to stay calm, or they will hear me," he said, retrieving the flask.

The cold seeped into him now that he was no longer moving. He tried to focus his hunter's sight, and a hazy stump-like stone high on the wall caught his attention. He reached up to feel for a hidden catch. The stone was as cold as ice and covered in divots the size of his head.

"Oh no," he gulped as the truth sank in. "Teeth

marks. They've bitten and chewed through solid stone—that's how the tunnels were made."

Sterling's stomach twisted as he imagined how easily human bones would snap under a troll's bite. Suddenly, the cave bugs didn't seem so frightening. For the first time, he thought he may not leave this place alive. It was a disturbing thought, but he pressed ahead.

His friend, the potion wizard, had spoken of night troll teeth and their power. The base of the wizard's staff was forged from a night troll tooth—part of one, anyway. And wizards were fussy about their staffs. Sterling was sure he was coming close to something important in these caves. He would not give up.

Mustering his courage, he leaped to put his weight against the stone button. A stone slab slid into a rough-cut pocket. He listened once more for footsteps of cave creatures but instead heard the distinct sound of a remarkably big set of lungs. He clutched his dagger and gritted his teeth. Sterling stepped through the doorway with only half an idea of what he would say to a night troll if it didn't bite his head off first.

"Welcome to the underworld, human. The Dark Forest was too tame for you?" a scratchy voice asked from the shadows.

Sterling strained to make out a shape—patches of a slender figure with a pointed hat.

"I'm here to speak with the Night Troll King," Sterling replied, trying to imagine what, besides a troll, might be lurking in the dark.

"As a young wizard, I never appreciated the art of conversation. But in time, I've found it useful," the voice explained. "What could a young thing like you possibly have to discuss that would interest the trolls?"

The being was articulate and notably nonthreatening. It bore a resemblance to his wizard friend who, in these very caves, he'd been thinking of just moments ago.

Uncle Roag's warning sprang into his thoughts. *Night trolls can get in your head—they can use mystical mind-reading powers.*

"Show yourself," Sterling demanded. "And you can cut the imagery. You're no wizard."

Grunting and wheezing, the figure melted into a misty soup before reforming into a bulky mass—with no wizard cap this time.

"You are wiser than most, but that won't save you. Your bones will be a welcome addition to my necklace," the figure boasted. He stepped forward, and with a snap of his fingers, a wall torch blazed with vibrant green-and-yellow flames. It popped and snapped as if it detested the damp cave as much as Sterling did. Nonetheless, it cast a deep green light, revealing a night troll. Its mouth stretched in a gruesome smile, revealing two sets of four teeth—each bigger than Sterling's head—wedged between wicked fangs.

The troll's skin was covered in ragged scars and leathery skin the color of a dead turtle's belly—sickly gray and smeared with dirt. Like the Troll King statue, a sprawling network of tattoos adorned the living creature's body. They were, in contrast to his other features, intricately beautiful, like artwork. Sterling surveyed the room. It was the shape of a flattened sphere, and there were no exits except for the closed door behind him. He had to buy time.

"This version of you is much more impressive. You should have started with the truth," he quipped.

The troll snickered as one eye fixated on Sterling and the other, a glowing orange orb, flickered with a strange flapping noise.

"How many others are you calling to fight me?" Sterling guessed, trying not to let his hopelessness leak into his voice.

"Very perceptive. But they are not coming to fight you. They are coming to clear away our very hungry pets once they've picked the meat from your bones. I told you, your bones will hang from my neck, and patience isn't in a troll's blood."

Before Sterling could craft a smarmy response, the rumpus of flailing insect legs grew to deafening levels. Sterling's ears throbbed, and he struggled to coax both his blood magic and hunter's senses to work together. Cave bugs streamed into the room, clattering along the ceiling. One of them snipped a chunk of Sterling's hair, but a hidden door crashed open, and a young foul-smelling troll swatted the bug aside.

"Leave the human until *He* commands otherwise," a female troll ordered as she followed the young troll into the room. She glared down her nose at Sterling. "Why have you come here? Do you have a death wish or just wanted to see the cursed night trolls for yourself?"

Think, Fierce. You came here for answers. You can't fight your way out of this one. Talk your way out, he convinced himself.

"I thought I could find a troll skeleton lying around—your bones and teeth are powerful weapons against the dark elves. Do you know of the war coming to Everen? It's not too late to join the fight against the dark elves," he blurted out, trying not to sound desperate.

"There's no fighting the dark elves," the young male troll snapped.

"Our kind stood against them long ago and look what became of us!" the female retorted. "Banished from the sun, never to feel its warmth. Our young grow in the shadows, never knowing a blue sky. They have cursed us." She stepped forward, jabbing her spear toward Sterling. "What would you do if you did get your hands on a night troll tooth?"

"I'd fight—destroy as many dark elves as possible," he replied honestly.

The leader groaned. "That boring plan leaves me without a new necklace."

"And it doesn't help our curse," the other male growled.

"Every curse has a cure. If you help defeat the dark elves, I promise I will help you find a way to break your curse. The Everen elves are fair, and I've seen firsthand the healing magic Queen Clarelle possesses. It's worth the risk—to be free—to walk in sunlight again," Sterling pleaded, thankful when his sense of smell faltered.

The female thumped away, locking eyes with her leader. They exchanged grunts that he couldn't make out, followed by the female smashing a handful of smoke bombs against the ground, sending the thorned insects fleeing from the room. It was just Sterling and the three trolls.

"The human has forbidden knowledge. Could he be the one destined to save us?" she demanded. Her nostrils flared, and her giant eyes glowed pale orange in the smoke, challenging the king.

The leader puffed his chest and snarled, and Sterling didn't need to know trollspeak to understand the aggressive words. The female roared back, but her grunts were more desperate. The Troll King shoved her aside.

"There is nothing special about him. His skull will crack open with mushy bits like all the others. He isn't here to help anyone but himself. Get on with it and kill him."

CHAPTER THIRTEEN
A HARD DECISION

I f the circumstances had been different, he'd have chosen a different next move. Taking advantage of the tense moment and smoky air, blood magic burst from Sterling's veins forging a brute crossbow worthy of the troll's size. He'd held on to an image of a dark witch so powerful that he summoned his blood magic instantly. More blood shot out of his body than planned, depleting his body, and dizzying his mind. He forcefully straightened his posture and tilted his chin up, refusing to show any sign of weakness. But at any moment he felt he would topple over.

"Well, that's a delectable trick. I'd enjoy your company if I didn't despise the sun-stained skin on your privileged bones," the troll leader said through clenched teeth, surveying the weapon as if it were only a mild threat.

With only one arrow in his arsenal, Sterling knew

he couldn't simultaneously aim for all three trolls. The blood-forged crossbow hung in the air, switching aim at whichever troll stepped closest to him, to the amusement of the trolls. The weapon flickered as venom twisted through it, and the trolls chortled. Insect legs clicked overhead. Sterling's powers were meant to fight witches that went bad, not underground beings in their own home. He tried to plan a way out, but his thoughts were fragmented. Troll laughter echoed off the stone walls and vibrated deep into his skull. Holding his dagger in his nondominant hand, he realized his other arm had gone completely limp from the poison.

Things had gone from bad to worse.

"I did not come here to fight you. I came for your help," he explained.

The smoke in the air settled, and he surveyed the three agitated trolls encircling him. The young one was trying to circle behind him so that he couldn't aim his weapon at the king without leaving his back vulnerable. The female stepped forward, thrusting her spear between Sterling and the king defensively.

"You don't have to do this—we can help each other." He finally made eye contact with the female troll. Her gaze shifted questioningly to the king, then lowered deferentially—or was that guilt?

Bug stomachs gurgled overhead, and insect legs clicked. Sterling activated his dagger with a fiery blaze of red flames and aimed his crimson crossbow between the leader's eyes.

"Think carefully," the Troll King taunted. "You can't attack us all. Decisions can be *so* hard." He hefted his spear.

Suddenly, Sterling's mind cleared, and he knew what he had to do.

The young troll growled impatiently and jabbed Sterling's gut with the blunt end of his spear. Cave bugs leaped from the ceiling, but Sterling concentrated on his crossbow. He would only have one shot. The weapon repositioned itself toward the leader's heart before abruptly pivoting straight up.

"Now!" he commanded.

The trigger snapped, blasting the blood arrow into the cave ceiling. Shards of rock, mud, and dislodged insects plummeted in every direction. The trolls roared in fury, and the female's eyes widened as the king tried to swipe debris from his eyes. She hefted her weapon, and Sterling took a step back, but she leaped toward the king, plunging her spear into the center of his chest. A violent scream rang out, shaking the enclosed tunnel. The leader thrashed and bucked, crashing to his knees before face-planting onto the cold, rocky floor. Blue blood gushed out of him as the female rolled him on his side, retrieving her spear with one strong pull.

With the king no longer a threat, Sterling dropped to the ground like a sack of pecans, drained from expending his blood magic at such a high quantity. He whistled to it to return, mistakenly drawing the young troll's attention.

"You did this!" he roared and lunged, jaws wide.

Sterling clutched his fiery dagger but did not strike. Instead, he closed his eyes and hoped with every fiber of his being that his instincts had not failed him. The sound of the female slapping her hand against the troll's chest was a motherly gesture.

"Leave him. This is my choice—the human sensed that the king's mind had rotted. He has conceived of a better future. It is time for a new leader of the night trolls. Reborn is our hope and a chance for us to walk in the sun as our kind once did," she explained.

"You trust this human with our future?" the young troll blurted.

"I have to try," she said, nodding at Sterling. "He has trusted us already with his life. The light in him shines brightly. I want that brightness for you, my son —for our kind. We have suffered long enough."

Sterling gulped and tried to exude confidence. How quickly would they bite off his head if he didn't make good on his promise? But he knew one thing for sure, out of the present options, partnering with night trolls was the least terrible, and perhaps it would lead to something greater.

"We have a better chance together," he nodded confidently, watching her pluck the bony crown from her former king's head and place it on her own.

The female chanted in her native tongue over the lifeless body before yanking the largest tooth from his mouth.

"Here, a token of our alliance." She tossed it to

him, and he stumbled under its weight. It was as long as his forearm and coated in a slick mixture of troll spittle and blood.

The insects scurried out of sight at their new queen's command, and Sterling gripped the gnarly tooth, dripping with blue ooze, with thanks.

"Come," the Troll Queen said gently, and Sterling followed mother and son through a hidden door and up a gentle incline. Soon, an outline of hazy light revealed a doorway at the top of a tunnel.

"This is as far as we can go until nightfall. Here, take this," the Troll Queen said, bending down to hang a leather necklace around his neck. She tapped a cone-shaped crystal drooping from its center. "Portal juice. It's an ancient formula—good to transport one fully grown troll to one destination anywhere they wish. But you are much smaller. I'd imagine you could travel to several places with just this. Just picture the place clearly as you sip. Use it wisely. Save the last drop for the battlefield. Once it is empty, the crystal will lead us to your location. We will know it is time to join you. We will be ready to fight the dark elves."

"Thank you. Um—I don't even know your names."

"I am called Anthrah. And this is Banthtel."

"I am your ally until you prove unworthy." Banthtel pounded the bottom of his spear against the cave rock.

"Sterling Fierce," he said with a slight bow. "I hope to stay worthy."

CHAPTER FOURTEEN
THE GREAT OUTDOORS

As soon as he took his first gulp of forest air, Sterling knew he'd escaped certain death. He dropped to his knees in the soft dirt and leaves. The outdoors had never felt more like home. Scanning the trees, he realized he was nowhere near where his uncle would be waiting for him—but he knew this place.

"This is the old home of the elves," he said, standing. Around him, once-majestic trees loomed into the dark night, offering hints of Elvish craftsmanship, now tarnished and overgrown with rot and weeds.

He brushed off flecks of golden leaves from his pant legs and swished away tiny glitter flies from his troll tooth. Eager to be on his way, Sterling plucked the glass bottle from around his neck, only now realizing he wasn't sure how to use it.

A familiar voice called a greeting. Sterling tucked

away the potion amulet as his uncle appeared in the glow of his insect-powered lantern.

"How'd you know where I'd be?" Sterling asked. Banefield snorted a greeting. The young hunter was astride his stallion in a moment, troll tooth safely stowed in a large saddlebag.

"You don't get to be a decent mapmaker without knowin' how to read the signs o' the land," Uncle Roag replied.

"You put a tracker on me, didn't you," Sterling snorted, thinking more clearly in the fresh forest air.

"You betcha. I used an ingredient from fairy ale, a rare flower's nectar. Then, I used a nectar fly to—um, you don't wanna hear the details right now, do ya?"

"Not in the slightest," Sterling said with a smile. His hand brushed the pocket containing Evenna's pearl, and his mind filled with the image of a shadowy figure over a petite bed. Sterling lowered his hand and tried to clear his vision. His blood pulsed then settled, allowing his hunter vision to activate.

Uncle Roag was scanning the darkened trees. "We best be on our way—I know a shortcut outta these woods."

The pair weaved through the maze of midnight-dark trees. They rode hard, cloaked in shadows like the rest of the Dark Forest. At the brink of daylight, they reached the border between the Dark Forest and the Swamplands.

"We're safe from the likes of dark forest creatures

and night trolls here," Uncle Roag spouted with pride. "I can feel the sunlight in my beard! Where to next?"

"We don't have to worry about night trolls anymore. At least, I don't. You see—" Sterling stopped, realizing he didn't have time to explain the alliance with the night trolls.

Banefield's hooves struggled to free themselves from the mud and sludge beneath them.

"I see what?"

Sterling shook his head. "We need to get through the Swamplands. I've got a troll tooth now, and I think I know someone who can help me make the best use of it. The only problem is, Banefield's horse-shoes have always helped us gallop over the water. I'm not sure how deep it goes—Midnight may not be able to cross it."

"Nothing this big boy can't handle," Uncle Roag retorted with a cheery grin, patting his horse's shoulder. "Now, that's a nasty gash you got there."

Sterling hadn't felt the trickling of puss oozing from his facial wound. But a quick swipe of his fingers revealed it was getting worse—likely infected, but that side of his head had gone numb. He'd nearly forgotten about it.

"It'll have to wait," Sterling said softly, holding the reins firm as he tried to focus his blood magic on the wound. It twisted out of his control, and sudden pain flared from his wound all the way to his fingertips.

Uncle Roag gave a discontented grunt but rode on. Soon, the swampy water rose to the horses' chests.

Any trace of solid land had softened to muck, and moss floated across the water's surface speedier than the horses could move forward. Sterling whispered in his horse's ear. Banefield nodded in agreement and clicked his enchanted hooves beneath the murky water. Blue lights flicked on, one under each hoof, lifting the horse and his rider to hover over the water.

"C'mon, hand over the reins, and I'll pull you to the forest's edge. Maybe we can go around," Sterling suggested.

His uncle huffed, and his forehead glistened with sweat. He looked more worn than he had in weeks.

"Everen's stars, Sterling, I can't go faster. My supply o' special juice got nabbed in the forest. Some lil' goblin made off with my satchel when I was doin' nature's business. The pocket-sized thief laughed for miles. I don't want to slow you down. I'll slip through the Dark Forest and ride to Lornia, then Bren—to warn them and the other villages about the dark elves' ghost soldiers poaching blood beetle dig sights. You go find Evenna," he wheezed, tossing Sterling a half-empty bottle.

"The last of your healthy juice? I can't take this," Sterling rebuffed.

"Hurry and clean out that gash in your face before it worsens. It'll help stave off the infection but won't make it look any prettier," Uncle Roag said with a twinkle in his warm emerald eyes.

Sterling's head lowered as he tugged Midnight toward the Dark Forest. As much as he wanted to convince his uncle to go with him, he knew there wasn't a way. He poured the syrupy blue goo over his cheek. The mixture tingled, and sensation returned to his arm and fingers. The pain diminished, but the toxins still battled his blood magic, throwing him off balance.

Uncle Roag made him promise to be careful before slipping into the forest's shadows. Sterling thanked him for his help, and that seemed to make his uncle happy. Yet as he watched his uncle ride away into danger, a hollowness panged in Sterling's chest.

Sterling rode south, gliding over the Swamplands thanks to Banefield's enchanted shoes. The sky went from a stunning blue to sunset orange as he followed the Great River to the Sea of Grunne. Stars winked into sight overhead, and after nearly toppling off his horse, caught in an unexpected doze, Sterling decided to take a brief rest where the land met the sea. His urgency pressed on him, and after the shortest rest he could manage, he once again climbed into the saddle and set out over the sea toward the nameless islands. He embraced the familiar salty air blowing against his face. Splashes of cold ocean soon soaked his pants and boots, but the scent of horse sweat and seawater comforted him, forcing him to focus only on riding through the night.

A thin layer of silver fog rose from the sea, hazy in the light of a full moon. Beneath it, a patch of deep green appeared, soon revealing itself as a thick grove of evergreens surrounded by rocky shores.

"C'mon, Banefield, we have a wizard and a meute to bother," he said. He was excited to see his magical friends again, even if his visit wasn't a social one.

At last, Banefield reached the safety of the ring of trees and paused to let Sterling unsaddle him. Sterling wrung out his cape over a patch of wildflowers. The heavy droplets plunked onto the fuchsia petals, and the flowers turned their heads toward him, as if preparing to speak. He bent, breathing in their spicy scent and wondered if there was more magic in the world now or if his senses simply detected it better.

There was a thud, and Sterling scrambled to retrieve Evenna's pearl, which had gotten loose from his pocket. He snatched it before it was lost to the floral carpet below. He tried to send her a quick question in mindspeak, but there was no response. The pearl itself only added to his anxieties—it looked bruised. Its gleam had faded, as if the light magic had rubbed off. In its place, a dark purple gem was revealed.

Sterling tried not to correlate the condition of Evenna's pearl with her real-life state. He couldn't bear the thought of her turning dark. His blood thrummed at the thought, and a sudden spike of dizziness washed over him as toxins oozed through his body. Sterling stumbled to Banefield's side and clung to the horse, stroking his damp neck until he could wrestle his blood back under control.

"Okay, buddy, I'll be back. You know the drill," he

said in an authoritative voice, but it was more to calm himself than anything.

Before long, he was peering into the cave's entrance, searching for any sign of the potion wizard or his tiny companion. But the dark hollow was quiet except for the incessant drip-drop of cave moisture splashing against the icy cold rocks. Waiting impatiently, he thumped his boots against the cave's mouth, loosening clumps of sand and mud from his soles. Suddenly, a pop of purple light danced inside the cave.

Sterling perked up. "Good. He's awake."

CHAPTER FIFTEEN
RETURN TO THE NAMELESS CAVE

Descending into the cave, Sterling braced himself against cold boulders. His boots slipped where the cave drippings had puddled then frozen in sloshy layers. The last time he'd been a visitor here, he'd had the help of a flying dragon or levitating wizard. This time, he instead had toxins in his blood and the bad news of a powerful light witch in trouble. Eventually, he slipped around to the edge of a huge boulder and squeezed through a gap into the main cavern, carefully avoiding the witch eye in a jar that immediately zeroed in on him. His blood magic pounded nevertheless, but it wasn't reacting as strongly as he was used to. Sterling didn't have time to ponder this sudden weakness.

"Was that you making a racket out there, Sterling? I smelled a horrific odor—should have known it was just you. All this incessant potion-brewing clogs my nose," remarked a tiny tree-shaped creature with a grouchy expression.

"Hello to you too, Barath. I've missed your cheerful demeanor," Sterling retorted with a grin as he crouched to pat the tree.

Barath swiped Sterling's hand playfully with his branches and waddled toward a tall, slender figure in a pointed cap. The potion wizard steadied his half-moon glasses and studied the young witch hunter.

"Ah, yes, the birds told me a scraggly human was coming here by moonlight. You climbed much faster than before, Sterling Fierce. It is good to see you." The potion wizard scooped Sterling into a hug, his long beard tickling Sterling's neck. The hunter took a deep breath, enjoying the familiar scent of pipe smoke with a hint of baked metal, a one-of-a-kind scent for the most unique magic doer he knew.

"I've missed you both," Sterling admitted, swirling Evenna's pearl between his palms.

"You've grown taller. Your blood magic is undoubtedly more powerful if you've continued your practice. Well, you're in too much of a hurry for this to be a friendly visit. Is this to do with the Elvish war?"

"What can you tell me about the war?" Sterling blurted, shifting the weight of his bulky satchel to the other shoulder.

Silvery eyebrows arched. "How about I show you something instead? Stand back." He flicked his wrist, and his fingertips illuminated with a purple-blue glow.

Sterling leaped backward until his back thumped against the cave wall. He'd learned long ago that when magic doers say to stand back, they mean it.

"Here we go again. He's been anxious to show someone his collection. It gives me the creeps," Barath groaned and scratched his sausage-shaped tree bark nose.

With a swish of the wizard's wrists, purple light spread to the far corners of the cave. It revealed enchanted translucent barrels that faded in and out of form. Sterling squinted until his hunter sight focused. Blue liquid was stored inside. It looked like the drink Uncle Roag had called his "healthy juice."

"Do you know what this is?" the potion wizard inquired.

Sterling shook his head no.

"No doubt you are collecting blood beetles like the rest of us. But do you know why they are such powerful weapons? This beetle species carries a unique composition of chemicals or toxins inside its blood. They aren't toxic to you or me or tiny, ill-tempered trees," the potion wizard said with a wink.

Barath crossed his branches and turned away, mumbling about wizards and unnatural magic recipes.

Sterling interjected, "But they're toxic to dark elves."

"In a way, yes. Blood beetles or boomerang beetles,

as they were known in ancient times, can capsulize dark energy and produce a counter agent capable of destroying their attacker. If a dark magic doer attacks, then a boomerang effect occurs, sending dark magic back to its source. They also have divine health benefits if consumed by a caretaker of Everen's creatures or plants. Again, the boomerang effect—good deeds and compassion are matched by great rewards and healing. Of course, their power is activated only by enchantments—light magic and such. These beetles appear during times of turmoil and disappear for centuries at a time. When I saw them growing in number, I knew something was coming—there was a reason we'd need them."

"I'm not sure I understand how they work," Sterling said, scratching the scab forming across his face. His uncle's healthy juice was made with blood beetle essence, and it had certainly sped up his healing, but didn't seem like a promising weapon.

"Barath—name an enemy and their signature attack," the wizard insisted.

"Here we go again. Alright—I pick a bewitched swamp goblin using death breath."

The potion wizard conjured a swirling green cloud in the form of a goblin seething with black saliva. The wizard opened a small bottle of blue juice as dark magic began to rage within the apparition. Beetle juice rose from the bottle's top, forming a mist in the air. The potion wizard waved the goblin on to attack Barath.

"I hate this part!" the meute squealed, holding his leafy branches before his face.

Seconds later, the goblin's infamous yellow death breath was ballooning toward the potion wizard. Sterling pulled his cape to shield his face, but before the wizard began to choke on the cloud, blue smoke rippled around him. When it thinned, the goblin was nothing more than a few fried green sandy bits.

Barath patted his trunk body down but found no injuries.

"Do you see? The beetle blood detected the goblin's dark energy and countered it, quite effectively, I'd say. Isn't it magnificent?!" The potion wizard exclaimed, as the blue smoke retreated into the bottle.

Barath clapped his branches, slow and dramatic. "All hail the king of the boomerang beetles."

The potion wizard snorted.

"It is a respectable weapon against the dark elves. Do you think it will be enough?" Sterling asked.

"Of course not, but it can help. Dark elves are powerful. They draw their energy from ancient magic, like dark witches. And you know how dangerous that sort of raw power can be."

Sterling nodded. "Speaking of fighting the dark elves, I need your help enchanting this." He opened his satchel. The night troll tooth slipped out of his grip and rolled along the floor until it splashed into a puddle.

"Where did you find this?" the potion wizard

asked in a hushed voice as he ran his spindly fingers over the tooth's surface.

Sterling shifted with a sudden unexplained rush of embarrassment. "I didn't find it, exactly. I made a deal with the night trolls—"

"It is too dangerous to get into dealings with night trolls!" the potion wizard interrupted. "Their king will have your skull made into a decoration, Sterling!"

"I didn't have a choice. And I reasoned with them —her—the new queen. It's a long story, but we have an ally against the dark elves."

"There is no reasoning with trolls of any sort. You should know better," the potion wizard scolded.

"Doesn't your staff have a night troll tooth at its base?" Sterling raised one eyebrow.

"What are you not telling me?" The wizard squinted at him.

"A lot has happened since we last spoke. I rescued a white witch, a real one. She is half dark elf and half light witch—but she's on our side. It's just that the water sprites took her. If the dark elves have her, they may use her power against us in the war and turn her dark. I need a special weapon with night troll magic to have a chance at rescuing her. And I have to hurry."

"White witch? That is not possible." The wizard shook his head.

"It's more than possible. Here, look. She made this the morning she was taken," he lifted Evenna's pearl toward the lavender crystals that glowed along the ceiling.

The potion wizard wiped smudges from his glasses with his thick robe. His shoulders dropped as he studied the pearl's shifting colors.

"In all my lifetimes, I cannot say I have ever been so blind. Rumors—I thought the stories were fireside tales for entertainment, nothing more. She is dangerous, Sterling. You should have told me sooner." He pounded his staff against the floor.

"I'm sorry, Thahn."

Sterling lifted the troll tooth, wrinkling his nose at the pungent odor that lingered despite the quick rinse in the cave puddle. He deserved to be uncomfortable, to suffer, he thought. Sadness mixed with guilt. He had upset his friend. Only now did he understand that he'd neglected his friendships, too occupied with watching over Evenna these past months.

"Will you help me make a weapon so I can try to fix this mess?"

After a long silence, the potion wizard sighed. "Not every step we take would we choose to take again, Sterling. But only the wisest learn from their missteps to guide their path forward. Remember that, and I will help you."

Sterling nodded quietly.

"Alright. Now, start by telling me every detail that led you to the white witch and your time with her until this very moment. And I do mean every detail," the potion wizard said solemnly, summoning an enchanted tea kettle for his unexpected guest.

Sterling took a deep breath and began.

CHAPTER SIXTEEN
A STREAK OF GREEN

After some time and too many mugs of tea, Sterling assisted the potion wizard as he worked his magic on the tooth. It was cleaned, then soaked in different mixtures—a hot, acidic potion with a sulfuric odor clung to his nostrils, then a swirling violet and mint-green concoction bathed the tooth in a pleasant aroma. The final brew, fizzy and overflowing with turquoise suds, frothed then floated away like dancing stardust. As a result, the tooth resembled a polished white stone, ready to be formed into a formidable weapon.

"Now that we understand the gravity of your predicament, there is a question about which type of weapon to forge," the potion wizard remarked, tapping long fingernails against the tooth's sharp edge.

"I guess anything that would help me fight the dark elves." Sterling shrugged.

"A human fighting any kind of an elf is absurd," Barath snorted. "You have seen an elf before, haven't you? Best make a giant turtle shell. At least you'd have a chance to hide." The meute laughed so hard he coughed up splinters.

The potion wizard furrowed his perspiring brow and scratched beneath the rim of his cap.

"Now that's an idea. Would you like a shield? We have enough material to make a fine one."

"I don't aim to simply defend myself. The elves, like others, will underestimate me. I want to fight them head on. What about a battle ax?" he asked, puffing his chest and glancing at the meute.

The potion wizard strummed his fingernails against the tooth, more loudly this time, deep in thought.

"There's enough material for a weapon of that sort, though it doesn't suit a hunter. It's certainly not a stealth weapon, but it could do some damage—"

"No, you're right," Sterling interrupted. "A dagger, please. I've trained with daggers my whole life. There's no need to change that."

While the wizard searched his cupboards for the needed ingredients, Sterling sat with his back against the cave wall. The cold from it seeped into his core, and within minutes, he was slumped with his chin nestled into his chest, soaking in some much-needed sleep.

Hours later, bursts of bright plum smoke invaded Sterling's nostrils, and he jolted awake. After much labor, one simple yet unbreakable troll-tooth dagger was born. Its curved blade emerged from a double-notched handle. More sparks and smoke flew as the potion wizard weaved a spell into the weapon. A glowing purple light beamed from the dagger to Sterling, binding them. Wind blew across the cave's mouth with a whistling howl as the weapon's glow faded.

"My work is complete. The weapon and armor are bound to you, Sterling. Keep them well," he said. He slumped onto his floating stool and fanned himself with his cap.

"May I hold it?" Sterling whispered, noting that Thahn's eyes had shut.

He approached the worktable. The dagger's handle was slender but long, half the length of the blade, and chalky white. The sharpened edge was ghost white with a blued finish. It hovered slightly above the table, brimming with enchantments. To his surprise, a set of shoulder armor hovered next to the dagger. His hands tingled when he reached for them.

"Your crafting skills are like nothing I've ever seen before. Your potions are impressive enough. How did you learn to make these?"

The wizard chuckled. "If you've lived as long as I have, you have time to learn all sorts of trades. I must admit I have not forged weaponry for over a century. And armor, well, longer still. Oh, yes, one last bit— stay very still."

With a zap of the wizard's magic, the armor

floated to Sterling and fastened beneath his cape, each shoulder plate glowing as it locked into place.

"The night trolls are naturally resistant to dark elves' magic, so you have a formidable weapon and armor. Their teeth are reinforced with energy capable of biting an enemy's head clean off—be careful where you wave your blade," the potion wizard explained.

Sterling inspected the armor plates with his fingertips, biting back more questions. To be bestowed such gifts, especially from a wizard, was a great honor. Probing further could be an insult.

"Thank you. The armor is truly splendid. And the dagger is perfect," he said, holding it in his scarred, tan hands. It fit snugly. Then, something in his stomach tugged.

"Thahn, I'm sorry I can't stay longer, but I have to find the dark elves' fortress—it's outside of Everen's borders. Have you been to…distant places?"

"Yes. It can be daunting, even terrifying, to fathom other lands and kingdoms far from home. But they're truly there, and I fear your suspicions about the dark elves taking your white witch are valid. I know not where their fortress is, but it is rumored to be called Zaharen. I'd ask the dragons—it's likely a place they know and avoid on their travels."

Sterling nodded, feeling the heavy weight of truth.

"You will need a safe way to get there," the wizard continued. "The seas are too unpredictable in winter. I gather you already have a plan?" Steam coated his glasses as he sipped his tea.

Sterling smiled. "Green would know—he talks to dragons that must've traveled just about everywhere. I need to find him."

The potion wizard tapped his staff against the cave floor. It sparked a familiar emerald glow like the Story Dragon's scales. "I can call for him, but so can you. Look at your new armor."

At this, green light crackled along Sterling's shoulders, coalescing into the shape of a palm-sized dragon.

"Green! The imprint—it's him. The details look so real," Sterling exclaimed, grinning.

"It is real. A glimpse of him, anyway. Go ahead, give it a tap."

The electric green dragon zig-zagged across the shoulder plate until its face seemed to be pressed against Sterling's shoulder blade.

"Green! Can you hear me?"

One emerald eye blinked in return.

"I need your help. Can you help me find a place outside of Everen?"

Bright green light flashed inside the armor, and the dragon vanished.

"He's gone," Sterling said, smile fading.

"The bond you have with your dragon friend is threaded into primal energy. As long as you have that bond, this armor is a conduit between you two, no matter the distance. Don't worry. He will answer you," the potion wizard said with a yawn.

"I'm so lucky I can call you my friend," Sterling

admitted with sincere gratitude. He'd wanted to say it to Thahn for some time, and finally, he'd mustered up the right words.

But the potion wizard had drifted off to sleep. Sterling gripped his new dagger and exited the cave, searching the early morning sky for a streak of green.

CHAPTER SEVENTEEN
BEYOND EVEREN

L ike a magical emerald star, a dragon shape
swirled through the morning mist.

"Green!" Sterling called, eager to hug his
friend and rub the puffy cotton tufts of blue hair on
his head.

But the dragon shook his head, nervously
watching the rising sun as he floated in the sky.

"It's you, but you're not really here, are you?" Sterling asked as he checked his armor. It was completely
blank. The dragon was a light image that could not
speak or manifest a solid form. Still, Sterling smiled at
how mature his dragon friend had become. Dragons
aged differently than humans. The last time they had
met, he had been younger than Sterling, but now the
two appeared nearly the same age. It was not
uncommon for dragons to adopt humans as honorary
brothers. And Sterling enjoyed having a younger
brother, even if Green had never exactly been little.

Green's image flickered dull then bright again. Like anything pieced together by magic over a great distance, he would fade soon.

"Okay, I understand you don't have much time. Can you help me?" Sterling said.

Green held up one taloned paw. He turned his back to Sterling, whipping wispy clouds into letters that he presented to his human brother.

"You seek to go beyond Everen," the cloud letters read before they were carried off by the sea breeze.

"Yes, I need to find the fortress of the dark elves. I think they kidnapped Evenna. I need to get there."

Green's eyes dulled, and he stared at the sea waves crashing in the distance. He sighed and pulled more cloud pieces together.

"Zaharen is too dangerous. Even for you."

Sterling hoisted his troll dagger toward the sky.

"I promise I will return, and when I do, I will come to the emerald castle to see the dragon city you have built. I'm proud of what you have done for dragon kind and the alliances you've already made between dragons and humans. But it's my responsibility to go after Evenna. Show me, so I can do something to be proud of too."

Green appeared to sniffle as the sun's rays silently depleted the emerald lines that held him together. He crossed his arms, then shook his head in contemplation before turning his back once more. When he floated aside, a map hovered overhead. Sterling recognized Everen in the south, but several islands floated north and east of it.

"Which one is Zaharen?!" he begged, but his friend was already little more than a pale green outline. Two bright emerald sparks remained. One hovered over Everen while the other floated to the northernmost island.

Sterling tried to capture the map in his mind as the clouds began to shift in the wind. He tucked his dagger snugly beneath his leather belt and reached for the bottle the Troll Queen had given him. When he opened the cork, a strange metallic aroma wafted from it. He tilted the bottle into his mouth, concentrating on the island he hoped was Zaharen. Instantly, his body was pulled, squeezed, and elongated as it traveled through a portal with zipping lines of electric light. A whirl of colors spun around him so brightly, it felt like he had been sucked into an angry rainbow. Then, his body snapped back to its natural shape, and he found himself slipping through a clear tube. He looked down from a height he'd seen few birds fly to and tried to swallow his alarm.

"We aren't in Everen anymore," he reported, looking for Green in his shoulder armor. The image of a tiny dragon was nodding emphatically and waving its hands even as it dimmed.

"The seawater has changed—it's darker and deeper here," Sterling continued, hoping Green's magic was strong enough to maintain half a conversation.

Abruptly, the tube dipped toward a lone mountain peak encircled in a rust-brown mist.

"This is not Zaharen," Sterling spoke softly. "This is somewhere else. It's...familiar somehow."

He took a deep breath as a clear plate broke away from the tube beneath him, and Sterling plunged into the fog, gripping the translucent substance for any hint of control as it soared down. He braced himself, descending toward the isolated island and activating his low-light vision.

"Stay right, and then half-circle swoop down. We can land near those trees," he said to the tube piece, unsure whether he could control it.

Palm trees whooshed by as sharp leaves whipped across his face.

"Not *those* trees!"

Sterling hacked up brown, soupy mist and suddenly found himself scrabbling for grip on a palm frond. The tubing had vanished. His body weight tugged the leaf from the crown of the tree, and Sterling threw his arms around the trunk as it whizzed past. He stopped abruptly, his armor catching on the rough ridges of bark. He took a deep breath, then slowly shifted his weight and began inching down the trunk. At last, his weight landed on hard sand.

"This is not a fortress—some kind of deserted island," he whispered, noting the thick fog. He clasped the teleportation potion, but bile rose in his throat, and he sat quickly, waiting for his nausea to pass. He decided he might as well explore on foot until his stomach calmed.

After some time and a few run-ins with the spiny foliage, an orange-purple sky came into view, and the fog thinned. The glow from the morning sun warmed his skin, and thickets of white-barked trees topped with blue-and-purple leaves populated the forest before him.

"I know this place," he admitted.

Instinctively, he felt a tug toward the trees. Once he reached them, the scent of his father's soap welcomed him. He followed the familiar smell until he reached the innermost depths of the forest. His hand strummed along engravings in pure white bark. Each design was unique, with wispy lines winding along paper-smooth bark like lost streams. Star-shaped leaves waved from above, the sound like silken fabrics brushing each other. Toward the mountain's base, his boots crunched on a light snowfall. The chill in the wind pierced his clothing, but his hunter's instincts pointed him toward a heat source. Weaving around a thicket of frosted trees, he tracked the warmth to a modest campfire. The embers glowed a lemony orange with hearty, purple-tipped flames.

"Who made this fire? There are no footprints in the snow," Sterling wondered aloud as he searched the grounds. Then, he had an idea.

"My name is Sterling Fierce, son of Sir Rider Fierce."

A wall of purple flames rose from the campfire. He

whirled away but slipped and landed face down. He lifted his arms to shield his eyes from the intense light. His forearms burned. But it wasn't from the heat. Droplets of witch-hunter blood strained from his arms, then abruptly gathered to form a giant hand. It reached out and politely knocked on a door made of radiant purple flames.

CHAPTER EIGHTEEN
UNWELCOME GUEST

The ghostly door of fire swung open, and Sterling's blood magic returned to his body. He squinted to make out a long, shadowed hallway inside the purple flames. A bead of sweat trickled down his brow, a warning that the fire, magical or not, was real. He squared his body toward the opening and leaped through the doorway. Heat pressed him onward, and he hurried down a corridor that resembled purple smoke.

All at once, another door opened in front of him, appearing so fast, Sterling had no time to hesitate before stepping out onto snowy ground. The door slammed shut and vanished in a puff of smoke. A sheer rock face rose only a few paces away. Snowflakes fluttered onto his face as Sterling craned his neck to gaze at the mountain peak.

Not for the first time, he regretted not asking how the teleportation potion worked. He fought off a wave of nausea. Between the cave bug toxins, his lack of sleep, and the residual motion sickness, he certainly wasn't thinking clearly.

Laughter echoed distantly off the mountain rock. He set off, searching the crevices for a cave opening or other signs of life. He clambered up a jagged boulder and into a hollow. Inside, he was confronted by a round stone door coated in algae the color of ripe limes.

"It's an entrance. But to where?"

He wished for hunter luck and shoved his weight against the door. To his surprise, the thick stone spun from a central axis. He stumbled through and nearly landed in a set of footprints he recognized instantly as his own. This was where he'd entered the fiery door moments before—but now, a murky layer of fog coated the ground, and the campfire was cold.

"Alphadors! At the ready!" someone shouted.

Sterling unsheathed his daggers and took a wide stance, a blade in each hand as his nausea roiled. He was surrounded by a trio of bipedal figures, two males and one female.

"He's spirited, isn't he?" one of the males boomed. Flashing an amused grin, the speaker withdrew a curved spear tip and pressed it into the snow so he could lean against it casually. The spear was taller than a horse, and the warrior was nearly as tall. His glossy blue skin resembled a fish's, and fluttering slits in his neck and chest hinted that he could breathe underwater.

Trying to keep his composure, Sterling scanned the two beings who still pointed their weapons at him. The female wore a feather headdress and snarled from behind a crossbow while the other held a slingshot at the ready.

"I am not here to fight you. I'm not even sure where I am—the portal took me here by mistake," Sterling said in a low voice.

The feathered one lowered her crossbow toward Sterling's legs. Her arms were peppered with down, like the underside of a bird's wings. The third figure stretched his slingshot, a spiked stone gleaming wickedly in the pocket. This warrior was short and wiry, and his skin rippled with spiked scales. He closed one reptilian eye to aim.

"What business do you have at Mount Dorien?" the feathered one demanded.

He guessed that each being had adapted the physical attributes of the animals they led or hunted. Sterling's lack of animal features made him an instant outsider.

"My name is Sterling Fierce. I am from Everen and am trying to reach Zaharen," he said calmly, lowering his blades.

The crossbow rose to chest height again. "A supporter of the dark elves is an enemy to us," the female snarled.

"No, the dark elves have attacked my homeland. And I have reason to believe they've kidnapped my friend. Please, I'm here to ask for your help—there's plenty of fighting waiting for me when I return," he explained.

"What makes you think you deserve our help, falcon eyes?" the fish guy sighed.

"Just activate your feathers and be on your way," the lizard grunted.

"Huh? I don't have feathers," Sterling retorted.

The female cocked her head and took a step forward, lowering her crossbow again. She glared at Sterling's weapons, and he sheathed the troll dagger, trying to seem nonthreatening but still capable of defending himself if needed. She lifted one foot, then paused, her motions reminding Sterling of a cautious pigeon. Then she was only inches from him, peering into his eyes, then at his exposed skin. He fought the urge to flinch away. When his hand twitched, she fluttered away.

"He's telling the truth," she reported. "He's no sky Dorien."

"Then why do his eyes look like that?" the lizard asked with an unnerving glare.

The feathered one shrugged.

"Well, he's here, isn't he?" the fish guy twirled his spear thoughtfully. "He passed through our portal, which means he has special blood. That makes him Dorien. But which kind?"

"He's surely not from the skies," the female grunted, slicking down her headdress as if disappointed.

"He's no scale Dorien. That's for sure," the lizard tutted, his forked tongue flicking past his lips.

"Nor is he one of my kind," the fishy one said with authority. "Hardly a surprise. Aquatics are rare these days. That leaves just one other. C'mon, let's get him to Bance. I'm sure he's around here somewhere being strange and unsocial as usual."

The other two finally put away their weapons, although Sterling didn't feel safe yet. They thought he was a Dorien, which he surmised to be a hybrid warrior with abilities of particular creatures. Once they found out he wasn't one of them, would they kill him? If not, they certainly wouldn't trust him until they could pin him with an identity.

The Dorien warriors led him back to the mountain he'd tried to enter earlier. Apparently its name was the Midnight Mountain. The aquatic one struck up a one-sided but polite conversation when he realized that Sterling didn't even recognize his people's proper name, Alphadorien. He briefly pondered Sterling's unusual features, but the subject of these musings was too busy memorizing the nearby landmarks to probe about the Alphadorien culture or history. He was already planning his escape if they turned against him again.

Once they reached the round door in the mountain's side, the aquatic one chanted in a language of grunts and howls. The door slowly swiveled open, and Sterling followed the leader, doing his best to shift away from the feathered one, who kept annoyingly close.

Thwump!

The scaled one had pounced on a small lizard and deftly flipped it into his mouth, swallowing it whole. Sterling gaped, but the feathered one prodded him with a clawed finger.

"Keep pace or go back Ellerah," she ordered.

"Everen." Sterling straightened his shoulders.

"Doesn't matter," she retorted.

"It would be respectful to call my homeland by its proper name," he clarified.

The feathers on her head rose, making her seem taller, forming a wide ring around her face. Short, black talons extended from her fingertips.

"Enough!" the leader commanded. "Freya, switch places with Randu."

She strutted away, feathers still standing on end.

"Let's see if falcon eyes can sprout feathers after all," Randu taunted. Then he was charging toward Sterling, spiked scales extended.

He stopped short of hitting a pole that was suddenly quivering between the two.

"You two are acting like inexperienced foundlings. Have you forgotten your training?" the aquatic one seethed, his gills flapping rapidly.

"Apologies, Tristen," they said in unison, lowering their heads.

Tristen marched toward Sterling, his face twisted in a scowl. Sterling gulped, and his blood pounded painfully. An iridescent arm reached toward him, but instead of making contact, Tristen merely plucked the spear from the ground and turned on his heel.

Sterling breathed a sigh of relief and relaxed his grip on his sheathed weapons. The foursome continued climbing through a circular track within the mountain's walls. Freya strutted farther behind, feathers still puffed out, and Randu skittered unpredictably along the path. But it seemed as long as Tristen was in command, Sterling was relatively safe.

He still flinched when Randu abruptly brushed past him to scurry into a snowy clearing.

"It's him," he hissed, flicking his forked tongue.

Sterling squinted and realized a hooded figure stood among the scraggly mountain trees.

"So it is," Tristen whispered.

CHAPTER NINETEEN
MEETING BANCE

"Bance, this Dorien came through our portal. He's not one of ours, so he must be one of yours," Tristen explained matter-of-factly, prodding Sterling with the tip of his spear.

The black hood tilted upward, revealing two blue flames where eyes should have been. They flickered against a hollow skull. Bance had no skin, muscles, or hair, just a chilling, expressionless stare. Black horns rose through seams in the cloak's shoulders, but little else was visible under its folds.

"Alright, Sterling Fierce from Everen Land. Here's your chance to make friends with a ghost Dorien like you," Freya touted. She crossed her arms defiantly, but the feathers sprouting from her skin fluffed up defensively, her anxiety evident.

Ghost? Sterling's thoughts raced through book pages and his father's stories. There had been talk of spirits that left the body and rhymes they'd sing about ghosts during fall festivals. But there were no ghost powers, ghost hunters, or even undead beasts mentioned in any folklore.

"Bance, we need you to evaluate him—quickly, please. We can't be away from the portal for long," Tristen reminded the crew.

The ghostly figure didn't move, but Sterling suddenly felt caught in Bance's inspection. Something resembling dark magic tickled his senses, and Sterling's blood slammed against his skin. Toxins, suddenly unleashed, rushed to fill the space, and Sterling swayed.

"Get on with it!" Randu growled, shoving Sterling toward the nightmare-eyed figure.

Sterling's cheek throbbed, and he plopped face down near Bance's boots. Nausea overtook him, and he was glad he hadn't eaten anything recently or it would likely have spilled from his roiling stomach. He managed to scramble to his feet as his blood magic, clearly of two minds, wrestled the toxins back under some semblance of control.

The ghost hunter didn't move, and Sterling's hunter instincts kicked in, scanning the towering figure. Now that he was closer, he realized that what he'd first taken for horns were actually spiked shoulder armor. The dark cloak fell to the ground, where it was shredded into tattered pieces, revealing well-worn boots. The top of a staff peeked over

Bance's right shoulder, strapped to his back and, fittingly, topped with a fist-sized skull.

Sterling didn't believe in ghosts. But seeing Bance made him question his beliefs. The ghost Dorien waved his skeletal hand over a torch planted in the volcanic soil. A serene flame as blue as the deep ocean flickered, and Bance lowered his hood. In the light of the flame, his face transformed. Pale green skin appeared over the hollowed bones, and the twin flames were replaced with wide-set but otherwise ordinary sky-blue eyes. Bance couldn't have been much older than Sterling—no wrinkled skin or beard.

"He is not one of mine," Bance said. "He is none of ours."

Randu stomped his foot. "But he came through the portal!"

Freya puffed her feathers and reached for her crossbow. "Impostor!" she squawked.

Sterling instinctively reached for his trusty flaming dagger. The blade glowed as he unsheathed it, and he regretted taking the portal juice. Perhaps the night trolls had tricked him—sent him far from Everen to this soupy island of aggression.

"Wait!" Tristen commanded. "His dagger is a hunter's weapon. That's how the portal let him through—take it from him," Tristen ordered.

Freya took aim at Sterling. "You are no Alphadorien. You should not be here," she said coldly.

"Hunters are banned from Mount Dorien for

deserting us when our worlds were taken. You will regret trespassing," Randu spouted.

"I tried to portal to Zaharen. If one of you could just point me in that direction, I will leave and never bother you again. Hunter's promise," Sterling tried to reason with them. He gripped his dagger with all his strength. Everyone froze when airy laughter floated through the clearing. Sterling's spine tingled.

"What's funny, Bance? You aren't going to help us get rid of this trespasser? Or was it you that let him into our realm in the first place?" Freya's tone dripped with accusation.

Randu rutted like an enraged mountain deer. "Yeah, he probably did this to spite us. Unwise choice, ghost."

This time, Tristen didn't command them to back down. Instead, his eyes dilated to a monstrous glassy black, honing in on Sterling. The spear leveled at Sterling's chest.

"We'll handle this without you, as usual," Freya sneered at Bance. She pulled the trigger, and a crossbow bolt sliced through the air.

Sterling's blood magic acted without him, forming a shield that absorbed the bolt. Thinking quickly, Sterling reformed it into a rope, catching Freya and Randu unawares. It cinched tight, and their heads clunked together. Freya's crossbow clattered to the rocky ground, and Randu writhed, unable to lift his slingshot.

The crimson rope flickered, then stabilized, now corded in greenish toxins.

Freya screeched. "It burns!"

Sterling's knees trembled, but he raised his dagger just as Tristen threw his spear. What remained of his blood magic roared and snatched the spear from the air, turning it on its owner.

Tristen gasped, and his eyes returned to normal, but his lung flaps twitched at an unsteady rate. He'd been struck by his own spear and turned his body to hide his injury.

Bance crossed his arms, revealing armor-clad fingers with wicked spikes on each knuckle.

"Too quick to anger, you three," Bance sighed. "And you, Sterling Fierce of Everen, you were almost too slow."

Freya and Randu squirmed. The poison couldn't really harm them unless it got inside their bodies, but it obviously was uncomfortable to the touch.

"What is he?" Freya squawked. "What magic makes blood weapons? Bance, you secretive skeleton, tell us now, or I'll command all the birds to peck your eyes out when you sleep," Freya demanded.

Randu snickered like a child laughing at an inappropriate joke.

"Tristen, tell featherbrain that I don't respond well to threats," Bance said in a low growl.

"Tristen?" Freya snapped, her skin prickling.

"I think he's hurt," Sterling admitted.

Tristen's slick skin was oozing with clear mucus.

Like a fish out of water, he gasped for breath. His lungs heaved in and out erratically.

"He's air locked! He needs to get back to the water," Randu snorted, suddenly concerned.

"Untie me! I'll fly him to the sea—hurry!" Freya shouted. Feathers poured out of her skin until she was covered with them.

Bance pointed the end of his staff toward the snowy ground. A jet of flame swept from it, creating a puddle at Tristen's feet. Sterling stepped forward, his blood magic forming a fist-sized cup. He guided it toward Tristen, splashing against his skin. Tristen took a ragged breath, then slumped to the ground, his breathing slowly returning to normal.

"Your magic smells like tree mud," Tristen coughed.

Sterling shivered and summoned more of his blood back beneath his skin. Warmth surged through his body, and he straightened, hoping that this gesture would be enough to stop the fighting. Bance nodded, his sky-bright eyes sparkling.

Randu's eyes darted around mischievously, but Freya was slumped with relief. She tested her bindings, eyes fixed on Tristen.

"Tell them what kind of hunter you are. They will believe you now," Bance whispered with a wink.

Sterling hesitantly commanded his thorned blood rope to unravel from Freya and Randu. The feathered Dorien rushed to Tristen's side as blood droplets floated back to their master and securely tucked into his forearms.

He sheathed his family dagger and slowly met each Dorien's gaze.

"I'm a witch hunter," he began, straightening his stance and speaking with confidence. "Bance is right. I have a quest, and I need your help."

CHAPTER TWENTY

INSIDE MIDNIGHT MOUNTAIN

"There's no such thing as a witch hunter," Freya squawked, rubbing the rope scratches around her middle. She sounded more skeptical than angry, which was a welcome shift.

Randu marched toward him.

"Can you show me how you did that trick with your blood?" he asked in the most respectable tone he could muster.

Sterling allowed him to inspect his forearms, but Randu huffed away, disappointed.

"I do recall witch-hunter lore based on real beings. What I don't understand is, if you're a witch hunter, why are your abilities not visible?" Tristen mused.

"When his emotions run high enough, he can activate his blood magic," Bance explained. "It's mostly visible in his eyes, which I suppose is similar to witch power. Did you see his eyes glowing? They flash gray —not black, but not white. He is the balance between dark and light power. His weapons are inside him, triggered only when he needs to defend himself."

Sterling cocked his head. He'd never seen himself while he was using his witch-hunting powers, and while none of this surprised him, he felt rather eager to find out what else the ghost hunter might know.

Randu snorted, mumbling a word that likely meant "nonsense," though much harsher.

"How do we know he's not a fake?" Freya chimed in, darting close to inspect Sterling's eyes. Her olive-green irises contained glints of gold, far more magical in appearance than his.

"I hunt witches," Sterling explained. "Their power is deep inside them so they can hide in plain sight— except for dark witches. You'd know one of those if you saw one."

"And I suppose your quest involves hunting witch-es?" Randu said.

"Well, sort of."

"Then why do you need help?"

Sterling opened his mouth to answer, but Tristen cleared his throat and clapped his spear against the ground for attention.

"We will take him to the capital. He will explain his quest to the brotherhood, and they will decide," he decided.

Freya and Randu exchanged disapproving stares,

but Tristen beckoned to Sterling, and the others fell in line behind them.

"I don't know if you should expect any aid," Tristen began apologetically. "Mount Dorien—that's what we call our capital—is more of a refuge and a stronghold. We don't often leave. There are four main races of Dorien, as you see represented here. Each was ousted from their homelands by the *Brethren*." Tristen grimaced at the word. "Together, we forged one collective race, the Alphadorien. And we welcome all Dorien types that suffered the same fate. As you've witnessed, we fiercely protect this place from non-Dorien—it keeps things simple."

Sterling nodded, and Tristen continued spouting tidbits of history. Sterling struggled to focus on the lecture as his blood magic squirmed inside and toxins twisted in his veins. Perhaps the Doriens would have a healer who knew something about cave bug venom.

Soon, they had arrived at a familiar moss-covered door. It seemed no matter how many times he went through it, Sterling would never get to the other side. This time, instead of opening to the outside of the mountain, the doorway revealed circular tunnels, extensively carved, that led deep inside the mountain. Eventually, natural light and the sounds of vibrant community life trickled into the tunnel, and soon Sterling was stepping onto a ledge overlooking a new land.

"Have a look around, witch hunter. This is the

home of Alphadorien," Tristen said, gesturing expansively at the secret world.

It was more immense than should have been possible, given the size of the mountain. His instinct was to believe this was a dream—an imagined place. But the vibrant details of the landscape and the scent of plant life confirmed it was no dream. The ledge he was standing on gave way to terraced fields that stepped gradually down to a spiraling river that pooled in four giant ponds, each surrounded with rows of fruit and nut trees. Beyond the farmlands, thick pockets of wilder forest rose, softening the rocky edges of silvery plateaus topped with pastel-hued plant life. Mount Dorien was about a quarter of Everen's size from what he could calculate. As his hunter senses regained their strength, the rich detail around him intensified. Flocks of sky Doriens in V formation soared overhead, and braided waterfalls flowed amid lively villages. The mountain rock glowed with embedded pink, yellow, and gold crystals, and a warmth hugged the valley like sunshine on a clear day.

"It's beautiful," Sterling acknowledged, inhaling the agreeable scent of mineral-rich soil and fresh water.

Bance tapped Sterling's elbow and motioned for him to look up. When he did, his jaw plopped open. Enchanted to float high in the mountain's center was a shrunken star, pinkish orange, the color of the perfect sunset.

Tristen's words faded in. "...one trade store, an armory that stays active day and night, three blacksmith stations, a food hut for each Dorien type."

"For obvious reasons, we prefer different food," Freya added, smoothing her longest head feathers, which shimmered a rich, olive-green hue in the warm light. She cupped her hands over her mouth and produced a birdcall similar to what Uncle Roag used.

Sterling hadn't considered his uncle since arriving through the portal. Memories of Everen felt distant. He slipped his hand around Evenna's pearl. This new world was enchanting, but he needed to focus on his quest. He tried to send the light witch some words of encouragement, but by now he wasn't expecting any reply.

"Well, we'd better move on. I placed a whirlpool spell around the portal, but it's temporary—we'll have to return to guard duty soon," Tristen explained.

"Where are your golden girls?" Randu demanded, thumping his scaled tail.

Ignoring her companion, Freya closed her eyes and took a deep breath. A gust of air announced a pair of winged creatures, each with a long, pointed beak and olive-green eyes to match their silky feathers. Standing at horse height, the giant birds hosted double-rider setups—leafy mesh saddles with dangling stirrups made of straw. Secondary feathers brushed against the ground as they landed, cushioning their sound.

"Two riders per Stelia," Freya said with a motherly smile at her feathered friends.

Tristen and Randu had already mounted the larger bird, and Bance hoisted himself on the other as he mumbled something about disliking heights. Sterling planted his boot in the delicate stirrup and steadied himself aboard the giant bird. It wasn't unlike riding Green, and he peeked under his cape at the tiny green symbol on his shoulder armor, wishing his dragon brother could see him. The tiny shape appeared to be reading a book but cocked its head as if sensing Sterling.

"Enfralla," Freya told the birds, which Sterling assumed was a command to follow her. Brandishing her own feathers, she spread wings of glimmering iridescent greens and flecks of gold. She smiled radiantly, resembling a goddess of nature, only missing a leafy crown.

The magnificent birds circled the top of the mountain before descending steeply, soaring over a marketplace full of trading, cooking, and chatter. Beyond that, a line of boulders encircled an isolated forest. Smoke rose from the branches. Sterling's hunter vision zeroed in on the trees, which had cracked bark, revealing liquid fire inside.

"I thought ever-burning trees were just a myth," Sterling shouted in the wind.

"Don't tell anyone here that, or they'll insist you touch them, and I promise that fire burns hot," Bance said indifferently from his saddle behind Sterling.

Tristen perked up. "Actually, the ever-burning trees were here first. It's said the mountain formed around them. Nobody knows how ancient they are or how long they will burn."

The birds changed course and dove toward the thick trees before Sterling could ask more. Wind whipped through his hair, and he bent low over the bird's back as the majestic creature banked around jungle vines and straight toward a waterfall set high in the cliffs. They didn't slow as they reached the wall of churning water.

"Hang on!" Tristen shouted as his bird shot through the waterfall curtain.

The bird beneath Sterling slowed abruptly and landed in the dim cave with a graceful bob. Sterling slowly unclenched his hands from the soft feathers of the Stelia's neck. Behind the waterfall, arched rock formed a domed room. Somehow, Sterling wasn't drenched. None of them were, and the birds' feathers were dry.

"Enchanted waterfall?" he asked.

Freya nodded.

"He asks too many questions," Randu snorted.

After the warmth of the faux sun, the cold cave air was unnerving. Sterling dismounted from his gracious sky horse—he preferred to think of the Stelia this way—and bowed to her. She nodded back, and once everyone had dismounted, the majestic birds fluttered back through the waterfall.

Using his night vision, Sterling scanned the cave.

There were no signs of any guards or council chambers.

"Over there," Tristen whispered, gesturing to a short pillar poised beneath a singular column of bright white light.

"Thanks." Sterling wondered how he had missed it on first inspection. His hunter's sight must still be affected by the poison. But his blood was quiet, seemingly in control of the toxins. He felt more refreshed than he had in days.

"Ah, snack time," Randu sniffed the air for mountain lizards.

"Shhh," Tristen hissed. "Don't offend the brotherhood."

Randu's forehead scales pressed together in confusion.

"He means don't eat lizards in their home, reptile breath," Freya teased.

"I worked too hard at becoming a leader. I'm not going back to cooking duty because you can't show some common decency." Tristen made a low croaking sound, tightening his grip on his spear.

Randu's tongue flicked in and out of his mouth nervously.

"He's right. The brotherhood would hold him accountable for your disrespect," Freya said in a hushed tone.

Sterling detected fear in their voices underneath the aggression. They feared the brotherhood, but why?

"Go stand in the light. And choose your words carefully—you only get one shot at this," Bance muttered, waving Sterling around the quarreling Dorien.

A queasiness settled into his gut as he approached the lone pillar.

CHAPTER TWENTY-ONE
THE BROTHERHOOD

S terling's eyes darted around the empty space surrounding the pillar of light. He glanced back at Bance, which was a mistake. The Dorien had transformed into ghost form, and his eyes glowed once again an unforgiving blue flame.

Go into the light, Sterling told himself. He was so nervous he couldn't feel the back of his throat to swallow, let alone speak. But he pressed on. If he could get the Alphadorien to fight the dark elves, he'd earn enough honor to allow his uncle to stay in Bren even if he were banished for failing to save Evenna. Unwittingly, he'd clasped Evenna's pearl with a death grip. Losing her was not an option worth considering. Yet with the pearl turning increasingly dull and bruised and with no answer when he tried to mind-speak with her, his hope, too, was lackluster.

Hesitating for a moment, he surveyed the beam of light. It was pure white, the color of moonlight, and it emitted a fairylike hum. If only he'd be meeting fairies —at least he'd know what to expect.

His body went on autopilot, and he watched his boots click into place, one next to the other inside the cylindrical spotlight. A low hum lulled him into a state of serenity as he stood in what felt like a cold ray of sunlight.

"Announce yourself!" A deep voice bellowed.

Sterling's eyes sprang open. The dark cave was gone, replaced by a brightly lit oval table. The background was hazy, like the inside of a puffy summer cloud. Nothing moved for a moment. Then, three ridiculously high-backed chairs formed, the tops reaching to the room's ceiling. Three white-robed figures shuffled out of the mist and took their seats.

"Well?" one demanded. There was a distinct flapping like the opening and closing of exterior lungs.

"I am Sterling Fierce from Everen. I've come for your help. My homeland is at war," he announced firmly.

"Everen is far from our island. Who is your attacker, and why should this distant squabble concern us?" the same voice inquired.

The mist cleared slightly, and Sterling confirmed that the speaker was indeed an aquatic. To the fishy man's left was a feathered warrior, and to his right, a scaled being. All three wore impressive crowns of glossy black obsidian.

"The dark elves," Sterling replied. "They've already sent ghost warriors. They've already attacked the

Everenian elves, a peaceful faction. Our allies cannot fight the dark elves and protect us at the same time. The dark elves are very powerful—" Sterling stopped himself before divulging information about Evenna.

The brotherhood turned toward each other and had a murmured discussion.

The leader turned back to Sterling. "What you ask of the brotherhood is too great a sacrifice. We will not take sides in an Elvish war."

"Please. The night troll's portal potion took me here for a reason. And the white-bark trees are familiar to me. Why else would destiny have brought me here?" he begged, spurring a flurry of hushed whispers.

"...Sir Rider Fierce..." a voice said cryptically, and Sterling's eyes widened.

"Witch hunter," another one whispered, emphasizing the word witch.

The leader lifted a mist-shrouded hand, and the others grew silent.

"There has not been a witch hunter on this island for some time. But hunters, in the early days, did come for training. Your ancestors' blood knows this place—that is why it feels familiar to you. The Alphadorien have been through enough war. We wish to live in peace, yet we need fighters like you to protect that peace.

"Fate may have brought you here to train as a Dorien, to open the passageway for other hunters to return. What we can offer is an opportunity to solidify an alliance between Dorien and hunters. But you must train in traditional Alphadorien skills first. If you are successful, we shall transport your hunter clans here to train and to live. Leave Everen to its war and join the Alphadorien, hunter. It would mean the survival of your kind no matter the outcome of the elves."

Sterling swallowed hard. He could save the hunters from the dark elf attack. But only the hunters.

"I want to accept, but I must—"

"You must decide in one day's time, Hunter Fierce. Return here tomorrow. *Obeau*," the leader said sharply.

The word made Sterling flinch. He'd nearly forgotten it. His father had sometimes said *obeau* when the hour was late. He used it to mean Sterling should go to bed—or else. Presumably, it meant "last chance" in hunterspeak.

Sterling blinked and found himself once again in a gloomy cave.

"What did they say?" Bance's voice rang out, his stout, shadowy figure coming into view.

Sterling shook his head with a frown.

"So, this was a waste of our time?" Freya huffed.

Tristen put a finger over his lips and glared at her.

Bance turned his back and took a deep breath. Seeing his chance, Randu dropped to a crouch, then snaked across the floor and snatched up a newt with his mouth.

Sterling explained the brotherhood's reason for

not helping with Everen's war and their conditional invitation to the hunters. The group listened solemnly. Tristan rubbed his face with one slimy hand. When he lowered it, he ordered Freya to take Sterling on a tour of the training grounds, then called Randu to return to the portal with him for guard duty.

Sterling palmed Evenna's pearl as a heaviness loomed over him. Despite a scenic flight toward the training grounds and an overwhelming curiosity to stay on Mount Dorien, he had no intention of staying to speak to the Dorien leaders the following day. But he couldn't simply waltz back to the portal—Tristen and Randu would never let him pass through on their watch. He could always use the troll potion, but he preferred to look for less unpredictable travel, if possible.

"Alright, we're here. I'll just go speak to—I'll be right back," Freya announced as they landed at the doorstep of an ordinary-looking hut enclosed by a worn wooden fence. Alphadorien moved about the grounds, some forming in groups, fatigued but committed. Others marched in solidarity with pensive expressions.

Those must be the trainers, Sterling thought.

A few Dorien spied the newcomer at the gate, nodding at Freya, who'd frolicked inside already. Although she received warm glances, no one shared the sentiment with Bance.

"Are they scared of you?" Sterling asked bluntly.

Bance sighed as he stepped into the fence's shadow, his blue-fire eyes burning.

"We aren't the most trusted pack for obvious reasons, and everyone's been fighting over my share of the mountain since I'm not using it. I'm sure you haven't noticed any other ghost Dorien here."

Sterling hadn't.

Then Freya was skipping back toward them.

"Okay, I arranged with a friend to get you registered quickly. They're expecting you now—Sterling, you'll be popular here. For whatever reason, they think witch hunters are something special. Anyway, I have to make a stop before going back to portal duty. Can you get him checked in from here?" Freya asked in a surprisingly sweet tone.

She soared out of sight without waiting for a response, but Bance nodded silently, tugging on Sterling's cape as he trudged toward the entrance gate.

"Wait, I'm just looking around the place. I can leave anytime, right?" Sterling hissed. He clutched his stomach, suddenly nauseated.

"I don't know. I've never been to training. I don't know how it works," Bance replied, the bones in his jaw grinding against each other.

"What do you mean? You didn't train with the others?"

"There are no others like me. I was the scout who found Mount Dorien for my people, but my world was lost before I could return to show them the way. Besides, I can't train with the other Dorien—my magic is…different." Bance stepped into the light, and his skin reformed.

"I'm truly sorry."

Bance shrugged.

"Um—did you say the others are fighting over your land? Maybe I can help with that—being an outsider, I could try to settle an argument," Sterling said, arching his chestnut-colored eyebrow.

"It's not that simple. The land was allotted to my people when I first came here, and it must be tended. I'd let the others use it, but something haunts my land —lizards, fish, and birds vanish after a few days of being set free there. They blame the spirits of my ghost tribe, but I know it's not them."

"It doesn't sound like you have a strong attachment to this land," Sterling noted. Bance met Sterling's eyes with a piercing stare, but he nodded ever so slightly. Sterling swallowed. "Can I go there to look around at least? I could track whatever is eating the animals, if that would be helpful. I'm a hunter, remember? It's what I'm good at."

Bance's hand, half pale green skin and half exposed bones, reached to open the gate that would lead them to the training master.

"You have less than a day to make your choice. Do you know what the brotherhood will do to you if you decline?"

Sterling's boots froze.

"Of course, I'm going to decline, and I don't intend on going back to find out. Don't make me go inside—

Bance, if I can fix this land dispute, would you help me escape?" he said in his best pecan salesman voice.

A flock of feather hunters flew overhead. For a moment, Bance was draped in shadow, and his eyes burned blue. His skeletal digits tapped against the gate's wooden boards.

"I hope you have a very good plan," Bance said as he released the latch, allowing the gate to slam shut.

CHAPTER TWENTY-TWO
BLIND TRUST

When Sterling put on the disguise Bance had constructed for him, he had to admit he looked like a rather gangly chicken. He chuckled at what his father would have thought of the whole thing. But his tangled hair was mostly disguised, and his telltale hunter's weapons were strapped out of sight beneath his cloak. Instead of checking in as a Dorien trainee, Sterling aimed to make his way through the various communities and onto Bance's plot of land, all while attempting to blend in.

Bance eyed him critically, then shrugged, telling him to stay in character even if no one seemed to be around. Birds of prey had very good eyesight. The pair scurried along side paths, staying out of sight as much as possible. The farther they got from the training sector, the less queasy Sterling felt. Despite his feather costume, Sterling began to feel more like himself.

Only a handful of hunters seemed to notice the pair, and those that did quickly averted their eyes from the blue flames under Bance's hood. Sterling narrowed his focus, stepping in sync with the long strides of the stranger he'd chosen to trust. It was a risk, but it was also his best option to return to the portal. The glass bottle around his neck was his backup plan—he'd take a drink if this didn't work.

Bance led him over the ring of boulders, balancing from one rock to the next with minimal effort. Luckily, Sterling's hunter agility returned to full force, allowing him to balance perfectly despite the slick worn patches in his father's hand-me-down boots.

Soon, they reached the fire trees. The crackling of embers filled the air. It felt like they'd shrunk inside the warmth and safety of a campfire. But soon, the back of Sterling's neck tingled.

"Do you think anyone is following us?" Sterling whispered.

Bance responded with a mixture of a grunt and a cackle.

"Did I say something funny?" Sterling persisted.

"Nobody would come near these trees, Hunter Fierce. It is forbidden."

Puzzled, he scanned the glowing tree bark and gulped as a set of eyes appeared. Elongated with pinpoint pupils, the tree's eyes twitched.

"Uh, Bance..."

"Don't make eye contact no matter what—just keep moving," he ordered.

Sterling was relieved to reach the other side of the grove but was puzzled to find himself in a familiar clearing. Were all the snowy clearings on the island similar, or was magic playing tricks on him?

"We climb from here to a tunnel inside the mountain that'll take us to the back of my land. Nobody will see us if we go quickly," Bance instructed, gesturing at a ledge high overhead. His cheek hollows filled with pale skin in the light of rose and amber crystals. It was a relief to see flesh fingers and facial expressions again—things Sterling had taken for granted before now.

Securing his footing and being mindful of his slick boots, Sterling initially kept up with Bance, who was a formidable climber. But the air thinned as they neared the peak. Sterling's progress slowed, and he tried to ask how much farther, but Bance had advanced beyond whispering distance. For a moment, Sterling gripped the rock with biceps burning, then he flattened his body against the cool mountain rock. He closed his eyes, hoping to regain strength and clarity. But instead, his head spun like he was in a dark whirlpool. In that moment, his hunter hearing detected a series of thuds below, and a shiver of worry spread over him. The eerie feeling from the fire forest returned. Silently, he pushed through the discomfort and up the mountain, away from the mysterious sounds below. Finally, he pulled himself onto the ledge and flopped onto his back.

"What took you so long?" Bance demanded.

"Sorry, I thought I heard something. I have a feeling someone is following us," he admitted, too exhausted to craft a more logical explanation.

Bance stepped over Sterling and scanned the mountain's face with surprising concern.

"If I'm risking myself for you, you need to move faster. You're under my watch—don't get distracted again," he scolded, lifting his gaze to the tunnel above with a stoic expression.

Sterling sighed in disappointment. If only he could explain how his instincts worked, Bance would understand.

"I know you don't have a lot of reason to trust me, but my hearing—"

"I am paying attention to our surroundings for both of us," Bance interrupted. "You are not ready to use your magic here—you'll only draw attention to yourself."

The words stung, insulting his hunter's instincts and judgment in one blow. Sterling bit back his response and got to his feet without a word.

They trekked inside the clandestine mountain passage and descended through a murky darkness lit only by the occasional smoldering wall torch. When the soft glow of pink light creased along the edges of a heavy boulder, Sterling gathered his confidence to see Bance's land.

"I'll be close. Go ahead and look around," Bance ordered, rolling the boulder to the side and shifting uncomfortably as he drew his staff from its holster.

The trees were white with lavender leaves, just like anywhere else outside the mountain, and the fog roiled serenely. Light snow crunched underfoot.

Sterling closed his eyes and breathed in the scent of mineral-rich soil, mountain rock, and a hint of decay. It was faint, and without his hunter's instincts, he would never have detected it. He pressed his senses to the fullest, despite Bance's earlier dismissal of them. He followed that hint of death to a dark hollow and knelt by seemingly ordinary shrubs. Tugging a few pointed leaves, he held them to his nose. His blood thrummed unexpectedly, and his senses dimmed, then returned in full force. What had been invisible to human eyes was obvious to his enhanced senses.

"Imagine finding you here!" he exclaimed. "It's okay, you can come out. I won't let harm come to you."

The foliage rumbled, and the ground shook. A distinct circular outline appeared as loose dirt sprinkled away from a mountain worm's face. The creature was pale white, eyeless, and as wide as two horses. She was not quite the same species as other giant worms he was acquainted with but still a welcome sight. He understood worms.

"My name's Sterling. The communities above your home are Dorien warriors—peaceful, but they've lost their home worlds. So they've come to live here. Do you know where their missing creatures have gone?"

The mountain worm mumbled.

"I see. Well, it's not your fault—nobody told you. But from now on, do you mind if inside the mountain, above the soil, creatures are off the menu? Outside the mountain is all yours—beneath the soil, please."

More mumbling ensued.

"That's very generous of you," Sterling said with a smile. The giant worm descended into the safety of her burrow. Sterling got to his feet. If only the Dorien people were so easy to reason with. In that simple conversation, a moment of mutual respect was had, the land would be "haunted" no more.

CHAPTER TWENTY-THREE
A HUNTER QUEST

"Are you mad?!" A screech pierced through the thickening fog as nightfall descended on the white-barked trees. Freya threw up her hands, feathers rustling, and stomped back to the fire outside the portal. Tristen and Randu shared scowls.

"Everyone, calm down," said Bance. "There's no reason we can't discuss it. Hunter Fierce did us all a favor." The skull on his staff pulsed an eerie blue light. "Freya, come back down."

Freya couldn't maintain a hover for long, and green-and-gold feathers fluttered to the ground as she landed. The feathers around her head spread out threateningly, and razor-sharp talons appeared at her fingertips. She squared against Bance.

"We are charged with protecting the portal. Hunters shall not pass," she said, reaching for her crossbow.

There was a golden glow around her. It was peaceful and warm, like the energy of the Lost Guardian Hunters tribe from home. Despite her hostility, Sterling saw hope in her.

"We cannot help others just because they are different from us?" Bance growled. "What good is being Dorien if you only do as the brotherhood decides? What about what we decide?" He raised his staff, pulsing with cold and powerful magic.

"I've already lost one home. I'm not going to lose another," Tristen said, gripping his spear in two moist hands.

Randu thumped the ground with his tail and grinned with a wicked look in his eyes.

Sterling stepped in the middle of the four warriors.

"Please, my friend was kidnapped by the dark elves. They will use her power in the war if I can't get her back in time. They will slaughter innocent people and they will not stop there. In hunter code, we look after one another," Sterling explained.

"We're not hunters!" Randu hissed, charging toward Sterling, baring a mouthful of sharp, yellowed teeth.

A ball of blue flame crackled toward Randu. His lizard eyes widened, and he dropped into a roll. Freya held her bow steady but didn't shoot. Tristen hoisted his spear, aiming at Bance. The skeletal warrior blasted three small fireballs. Freya flipped into the air and landed behind Tristen, and Randu burrowed beneath the dirt. Tristen leaped over the fireball and dropped into a crouch.

Freya's eyes widened as she realized she was standing in the path of Tristen's fireball. She squeezed her eyes shut, but the flames barely grazed the feathers of her forehead before it abruptly pinged off course.

Black smoke rose from the ground, and a blood dart zipped back to its master.

"Not helpful, Sterling!" Bance growled. Randu and Tristen rounded on him, but he buffeted them with more fireballs, and they shrank into defensive stances. "If they won't let us pass, we must defeat them. There's no going back. The brotherhood won't forgive this," Bance whispered.

"I may not be from here. But I know what being an honorable hunter is—and is not," Sterling said with conviction, rubbing his forearm.

Bance's shoulders dropped in defeat. Freya's feathers lowered, but her chest heaved.

"I change my vote to allow Hunter Fierce passage through our portal." She choked back a lump of emotion and avoided eye contact with Bance.

"You can come too." Sterling grinned boyishly, hoping his gut was right about Freya.

"It sounds like an honorable quest, but I cannot abandon my duties on Mount Dorien. If I left, the brotherhood would not welcome me back," she said mechanically.

"It's a big world out there, Freya. It's dangerous

and strange and scary and beautiful. You deserve to see it all, and you could help rescue my friend. We'd frustrate the dark elves and have a fighting chance to save Everen—there wouldn't be a boring moment." He smiled reassuringly before turning to Bance.

Freya's head lifted, her eyes gleaming. Then her gaze darted to Bance. Sterling took a deep breath.

"A hunter pack vows to protect one another. So no more fighting if she comes with us."

Bance tucked away his staff. "Us?"

"You don't have to stand guard here forever. What are you waiting for? Let's go on a quest—Tristen, Randu, we can all go."

Both took a step back, and Tristen shook his head "no" silently. Sterling met each Dorien's eyes in turn, then nodded to himself, trying to exude confidence. He would go alone if he had to.

This has to work, he told himself, swallowing down a lump of nerves and walking toward the portal before anyone protested.

The purple-flamed door flashed when he stepped through it, pulling him into a spiral of light. Moonlight flickered on ocean waves at the end of a short tunnel, and his boots crunched on cold sand. The brown fog roiled behind him as the flaming door slammed shut, leaving the beach in relative darkness.

All was silent for a moment, and Sterling pondered his next move. He didn't know how long he would have to wait. His hearing prickled, and like a cat on a mouse, he tracked the creature flapping overhead. It was swift and, to his disappointment, much too small to be his dragon brother.

"I wonder if Green got my message?" he whispered, staring at his empty shoulder armor. The dragon connection hadn't so much as flickered since he'd spoken to it hours before.

"It's beautiful beyond the mountain rock—the fresh air," Freya's voice came from above.

"Wait till you see the wilds of Everen," Sterling squeaked, unable to hold back his excitement.

"Well, I can't let her have all the fun," Bance's voice boomed from behind a trio of palm trees.

Sterling turned toward him and gave a hunter's salute.

"Again, tell me you have a plan," Bance insisted.

Sterling's shoulder armor tingled, and he smiled knowingly. Through the thick fog, an emerald-scaled dragon friend descended toward them.

"You're a sight for sore eyes," Sterling greeted. He made introductions, but Green was not eager to linger in the choking brown mist. Sterling and Bance climbed onto Green's back.

"He weighs as much as a pregnant horse!" Green whispered as Bance settled in.

"How?" Sterling replied, glancing at the skeletal figure.

Freya stretched her wings and surveyed the dragon's glowing crystal tail. She reached to touch it, and Green flinched away.

"Your tail is magic? Don't your wings work?" she inquired.

"Forgive them. They've never seen a flying dragon," Sterling said.

"I'm just glad I found you. Uh, bad news," Green spoke nervously, and his eyes flickered with dull amber within the usual vibrant emerald.

Sterling sighed. "There's no bad news, just challenges we must face. Out with it."

"War has broken out in Everen. The dark elves sailed into the Mirror Sea a day ago. The Vionin Kingdom was attacked first. If not for the Red Wolf, there wouldn't be anyone left."

Sterling rubbed the dragon's head. "I'm sorry."

"More will come. I'm glad you're returning to fight with us now," Green said.

A pang of guilt throbbed in his chest as Sterling explained they were headed to the dark elves' fortress. "But once Evenna is safe, I will return and fight," he concluded.

"Where did you say we're rescuing your friend from?" Freya squawked right in his ear.

"Does it matter?" Bance chimed in.

She rolled her eyes and fluttered away, confidently gliding in the sea breeze. "No, but I still want to know. Curiosity is a sign of intelligence."

"It'll also get you killed," Bance mumbled softly.

Sterling wondered if having both of them on this journey was a good idea. He didn't have much time, but if he could get them to work together, the chances of saving Evenna were significantly better.

"We are going to the home of the dark elves, Zaharen. We will need to stick together to make it out alive," Sterling warned, planting a seed of comradery, and hoping it would grow.

"Then we're guaranteed some battle wounds before we even *get* to the Everen war," Freya observed. "Who's this friend of yours who's worth so much trouble? I'd bet all my golden feathers it's a girl." One of her feathered eyebrows rose.

Sterling turned away, allowing the wind to cool his flushed face, and nervously stroked his nearly full beard.

"Evenna," Bance interjected, "is a white witch, half Elvish and half light witch. If the dark elves use her as a weapon, Hunter Sterling will lose the war—his home will likely be destroyed."

Sterling swallowed and nodded.

"What are we waiting around here for then?" Freya said.

They flew by moonlight as the ocean air blew strongly and waves clapped beneath them. Within a few hours, a dark blob appeared on the horizon. Sterling activated his hunter's sight to make out the shapes of thousands of intertwined trees. Together, the roots seemed to form the floor of the island, and deep within their twisted branches, stone roofs rose in intricate designs. Green swooped down, but there was little more to see than exuberant tree life and a short range of sharp-peaked mountains.

"This is Zaharen," Green spoke calmly. It was the dead of night, and even the stars looked dim and sleepy.

"You're my favorite dragon, you know," Sterling yawned, rubbing the tuft of hair on Green's head.

"Please be careful," Green begged.

"Hunter's promise. And tell the Red Wolf to listen for my call," Sterling said, preparing to jump into the mess of tangled trees.

CHAPTER TWENTY-FOUR
THE DARK ELVES' FORTRESS

G reen did his best to leave his friends in a safe place on the isle of Zaharen, but their sense of security was short-lived. The shore greeted them with snakelike roots and blocks of smoke-colored rock. Squeezing through a tightly woven forest of purple-bark trees, Freya, Bance, and Sterling crept toward the largest mountain.

Sterling discreetly searched the skies to gauge how far dragon wings had traveled, but soon he could no longer hear his dragon brother.

"I don't see a castle or anything. This can't be the right way?" Freya said.

"Not unless mountains grow candlelit windows," Sterling replied.

Freya squinted at the dark peaks. "I still don't see anything."

"If Hunter Sterling's instincts say this is the way, we need to trust him," Bance declared, which seemed to settle the matter. Sterling sent the skeletal warrior a grateful smile.

It was a slow, frustrating pace, maneuvering around swirly limbs oozing with a noxious sap, but Sterling felt happier than he had in a long time. They descended into an expansive thicket canopied with mossy limbs, tightly connected so that rain would hardly seep through in a storm.

"First over the trees, now under them? This place isn't boring, but it does reek like bad eggs," Freya said, pinching her nose.

"The trees are sick. It's not their fault," Sterling explained. "Dark magic will do that to living things."

As they pushed on, the dark magic grew denser until the thickness of it was hard to swallow. Bance, in shadow form, didn't seem to have a sense of smell, and for once, Sterling wished his senses would fade a little. But he refused to backtrack or choose a different route—not when they were this close to finding Evenna.

"I can't stay in this putrid pot of woods much longer," Freya gasped, eying the netting of branches above her as if tempted to break straight through to the sweet freedom of fresh air.

"You won't have to. Look, it's the Fortress of Shadows." Sterling signaled ahead.

The imposing structure's thirteen narrow towers reached the clouds. Starlight reflected off their glassy black stone wherever there was a break in the purple ivy that threatened to overwhelm the lower walls. The plant's sharp triangular leaves gave it a prickly, unwelcoming expression, topping its walls like icing dripping from the edge of a poisoned cake.

"What's the plan once we get in? How will you find Evenna?" Bance whispered.

"What if it's a trap?" Freya chimed in.

Squeezing the icy pearl in his palm, Sterling imagined Evenna's delicate face and silvery-blue eyes.

Sterling, they've done something to my magic. I feel weak...

Her voice faded, but the imprint of her energy stayed.

"She's here," he confirmed. "I can feel it." And then he could see it too. A beam of pale violet light the width of string guided him forward, and he didn't hesitate to follow. The glow disappeared and reappeared, all the while leading them closer. They weaved in and out of sappy trees, climbing over a jungle of rotted tree roots until finally reaching open space. Before them was a dirt path littered with footprints.

"These are recent," Sterling confirmed. "Keep an eye ahead of us, Freya. Bance, you're in charge of what may come behind."

Both nodded in unison. At least they could all agree to fight together.

Before long, the path trickled around the side of the mountainous fortress and into a forest of rusted metal cages. Giant blackbirds the size of horses were slouched inside. Rows of herbs, vine fruit, and vegetables rustled in the mountain air. And a modest storage house was attached to the rear of the fortress.

"It's not exactly waltzing through the front gates, but it'll get us in," Sterling announced quietly, proud of his tracking abilities.

"I've never seen this type of bird—they remind me of my goldies!" Freya grinned. With a graceful whoosh of her wings, she flapped toward them, cooing like a mother bird.

"Freya, can you please try not to excite them?" Sterling hushed, but two juveniles were already strutting inside their cages.

"Say goodbye to them, feathers," Bance urged gently. His heavy boots thumped over hay matted with bird droppings, which he ignored. He unlatched the main gate, and without a guard in sight, they slipped into the storage house.

It was filled with containers of birdseed and various vegetables, fruits, and some nuts that resembled peanuts, only larger. An unlocked pantry door led to a pitch-dark kitchen.

"Do you hear that?" Sterling whispered, desperate for a window and an ounce of moonlight. His hunter's vision chose that moment to desert him, and he froze as blood magic pounded behind his eyes.

Freya didn't seem to notice. "I don't hear anything."

Bance tilted his face, casting eerie light from his flaming eyes. It illuminated long, banquet-style tables piled with assorted fruits, stacks of round cheese wrapped in purple wax, and wine casks with snug corks in place. Freya helped herself to a handful of burtle seeds, and Sterling grimaced at the thought of eating the bitter nuts without sugar and milk. Freya crunched another handful before Sterling and Bance shushed her.

"What? I need flying energy in case we have to scram in a hurry," she hissed.

Sterling narrowed his gaze beyond the tables, and his night vision returned.

"Over there—Elvish servants," he whispered.

Freya swallowed, then tucked another handful of seeds into her pocket. Sterling led the way around the benches, careful not to wake several stout elves who were slumped over unprepared food or snuggled in the tablecloth. Sterling paused in the corridor to the main castle, listening for the guards, calculating their whereabouts. When he was sure the coast was clear, he motioned for Freya and Bance to follow.

For the first time, he felt the weight of responsibility for leading a pack. No matter what happened next, he hoped he wouldn't let them down.

CHAPTER TWENTY-FIVE
THE DARK KING

S lick walls lined the arched corridors of the fortress, radiating a dark energy. The stones appeared seamless, as if they'd been molded from hot wax. No cobwebs or dust from foot traffic appeared on the glossy floors, only warped reflections of three intruders.

"I don't like this place," Bance muttered, repositioning his hood to cover the light from his eyes.

"Me neither. It's cold," Freya whined, wrapping her wings around her body.

Spiraling into a maze of passageways only wide enough to pass through in a single file, they moved ahead cautiously, their path lit only by infrequent, purple-flamed wall torches. Soon, the ceilings shot up high as the passageway split into two directions, and Sterling hesitated.

"Now what?" Freya whispered.

The violet light flickered for Sterling's eyes alone, and he gestured. "This way."

This hall ended at a main area with black glass-like floors. Sterling paused in the doorway to inspect the fortress innards while remaining tucked out of sight.

The massive ceiling stretched to a single arched point in the center of the perfectly round room large enough to fit a village. Thirteen thick pillars created an inner circle and somehow supported the ceiling while also piercing it. Sterling squinted at the juxtaposition and realized that the columns were, in fact, the towers he had noticed from outside, but no matter how he focused on them, the architecture didn't quite make sense. He shook his head and turned his gaze to the far side of the room where a wall of barrels was stacked a story high. Guards patrolled the room and stalked the open halls and balconies that appeared at irregular intervals overhead, but most of the soldiers were posted near the barrels.

"So, that's where all the guards are at this time of night," Freya noted nonchalantly.

"What are they guarding?" Bance wondered aloud.

Sterling explained how the dark elves killed blood beetles in Everen to try to eliminate them as a weapon for light magic doers. He couldn't be sure, but it seemed these elves weren't above pilfering barrels of beetle juice, or worse, corrupting it. He was more worried than ever about his friends back home. The dark elves would do anything to win, which made them desperate—and more dangerous than he'd realized.

But he felt a warmth in his chest—Evenna was nearby. He scanned the thirteen tower entrances. One pulsed a violet glow from its door handle.

"We have to get to that tower entrance without being seen," Sterling explained.

"That's impossible. There are guards everywhere on the ground level, and who knows how many are posted above," Bance remarked.

Freya shrugged. "He's right. They'd spot us before we could get halfway across."

Suddenly, Evenna's voice echoed in his mind.

Sterling! You should not have come! Turn back—

Her words were cut off by a terrible scream. Sterling's whole body jolted, and his blood magic roared to life. That had been Evenna's voice...but somehow not. What had they done?

Freya narrowed her gaze at Sterling, sensing his frantic heartbeat.

"Sterling, it's not impossible for *you* to get there. We can arrange a distraction," she said calmly, nudging Bance with one wing.

"Shouldn't be a problem," Bance stated, sliding his staff from the leather holster strapped to his back. While his skeletal face remained shrouded in darkness beneath his cloak, his eyes glowed a more intense blue fire.

Sterling opened his mouth to disagree, but another gut-wrenching scream filled the tower.

"You brought us to help you succeed on your quest." Bance spoke with no fear in his voice, and the skull on his staff pulsed with blue light.

"Isn't this what a hunter pack does?" Freya sang, flapping her wings. She hooked her arms under Bance's armpits, and the two were streaming toward the barrels. Sterling allowed himself a moment of shock and gratitude, then raced toward the tower.

Evenna, I'm coming to find you. I won't leave you here, he said in his mind. There was a commotion of hollering guards as he reached the tower door. He rapidly worked his dagger around the hinges, loosening the door enough to force an opening. Sprinting up a tight staircase, he spiraled past what seemed like a hundred doors, one after the other.

Which door? Show me where you are!

There was no response, just another dizzying array of glossy steps lit by a minuscule flicker of yellowish light from moth lanterns. He was lost. He snatched the pearl from his breast pocket and squeezed it, trying to calm his breathing. The violet light flickered faintly, and he charged down the hall to an ordinary door made of purple wood. He drew his troll-tooth dagger and turned the handle.

Inside was a bare room with a round stone table just wide enough for Evenna's petite body. Orbs containing glowing yellowish-green caterpillars cast a sickly light over her body. To his relief, she didn't appear to be distressed. Instead, she was asleep. Gripping his dagger, he carefully made his way to her side.

"Evenna, let's get you out of here," he whispered, scanning her for injuries. All seemed well except for a bouquet of sharp, purple ivy in her hands. He picked it up to toss it aside, but wicked thorns held it fast, the needle-sharp spikes embedded in her skin and pulsing with a bruise-colored liquid. Her skin flashed periwinkle in splotches—contrasting her usual unblemished, alabaster color.

"What did they do to you?" He aimed his dagger at the vine.

Her eyes shot open when he grasped her wrist, but to his horror, their silver-blue hue and girlish charm had been replaced by infected purple that stared at him without emotion.

"No!" he screamed in shock. Pain gripped his middle with a crippling coldness. The air was thick with dark magic, and a beam of vibrant green mist twirled around Sterling's hands—pulling them like stretchy gum in opposite directions, away from Evenna. His blood magic begged to be unleashed, but he couldn't be sure it would leave Evenna unharmed in her current state.

"You're late, Hunter, but I am glad you made it in time to witness the final evolution of your *close* friend. Our young Evenna will be more powerful than any dark witch of her time," a voice creaked from a dark corner.

"Show yourself," Sterling demanded, using his hunter strength to bend his arms at the elbow. He couldn't wield his dagger, but at least he had some control over his own knife.

A tall figure with notable Elvish features stepped out of the shadows and advanced toward Evenna. He stood over her, caressing her hair where black streaks had grown amid the natural beauty of her once-ocean-blue strands.

"She has returned to me. It is only right that she be with her natural family. I am Eliad of Ohann, king of the dark elves, and Evenna is my daughter," he said smartly.

"You had the water sprites lie—she was tricked into coming here, but she wouldn't choose this!" Sterling proclaimed as hot tears welled in the corners of his eyes.

"She came of her own free will, desperately in need of someone to make the right choice for her future. Evenna was aimless, unsure of herself. I have given her confidence in her powers and a purpose. We will rule—together." Beneath the thick folds of his velvety cloak, he flashed a wry grin and met Sterling's gaze for the first time. Eliad of Ohann had piercing green eyes with white centers, and the look in them reminded Sterling of a predator that knew its prey was trapped.

There would be no reasoning with the Dark King.

Laughing wildly, brewing elbow-magic and troll deep

smile drunkenly at the King's Head

The mayor spoke to the doddering man below the

Dark King's dangerous embrace. He clutched his

wound in a grip... smiling Sterling heard the gasps

of relief reverberating from the chamber... pointing

at the bewildered mayor's... blood red of the head,

and then it was over, with that... troll-tooth at the

knee. Her field had an adequate... yes, united but

hidden.

Sterling felt the... even into their own clever... or a

moment and stared the... matches. For field I learna...

CHAPTER TWENTY-SIX
A DESPERATE LEAP

While the king spun his cryptic words, he hadn't noticed Sterling's subtle but strained movement. By the time the words had finished ringing in the chilled air, Sterling had managed to twist his hand so that the troll-tooth dagger was pointed downward. He held his breath, then released his grip with a silent hunter's prayer. The troll blade sliced through the emerald mist around his wrist. His knee rose as the dagger dropped, nudging it back upward with a spin, and it bounced into his other hand, cutting the magic in a precise trajectory. He clutched the dagger and turned his glare back on the elven king.

"Showy skills won't save you, not here," the Dark King cackled as his skin deepened to a shade like rotten plums.

"I'm not trying to save *me*," Sterling remarked,

launching his brewing blood magic and troll dagger simultaneously at the king's head.

The dagger struck first, embedding just below the Dark King's elongated cheekbone. He clutched his wound in genuine surprise. A crimson hand the size of a watermelon slammed into the elf's face, smothering his bewildered stare. The blood magic flickered and then it was twined with thick tendrils of toxic green. The king's enraged shriek was muffled but furious.

Sterling left his weapons to their own devices for a moment and seized the spikes that held Evenna's wrists. She gasped, then drooped into a deep sleep as he tossed the ivy aside. Collecting her in his arms, he dashed out of the green-lit room with a vine stub flapping against his cape and his blood magic still pouring bug toxins against the Dark King's face.

Rounding the corner, his head throbbed, and his knees nearly gave out from blood loss. Screams from the battle below echoed across the imposing fortress walls. He turned to call his blood, but his eyes widened at the sight of a bolt of dark fire blazing toward him. The crackling fireball gained speed. He could not outrun it for more than a short distance, less with the effects of anemia setting in. He turned at the nearest intersection and found himself outdoors facing a skywalk and a set of stairs that skittered around the outside of the tower. Pausing was a mistake. The purple-black fire lurched dangerously close. Sterling threw himself to the side, but the heat still grazed his shoulder armor, searing his cape. Dark magic pulsed. Sterling wouldn't be able to dodge the next blast.

He changed direction, sprinting along the skywalk and headed to the next tower. He knew not to turn around—every instinct told him to run. He pushed himself to run faster despite the fatigue that swept over him after losing so much blood. Closing his eyes, he felt each boot heave him forward but also sensed the bullet of fiery heat gaining on him. He focused on finding an outcome in which he didn't become a living torch. He burst through a doorway and came upon a shoulder-high wall. He clutched Evenna tightly in one arm and sprang to the top. His head swam and his arm trembled as he heaved himself onto the top of the wall. The fireball splattered against the stone at his feet and ricocheted up the arched ceiling. Several stories below, Freya whirled through black-tipped arrows, and Bance's blue fire exploded.

Sterling's chest fluttered as the fireball rocketed back toward his face.

"I'm sorry, Evenna. Best to stay asleep for this part," he muttered. He leaped for the nearest staircase and charged down several stairs before seizing the handrail and heaving his body over. He swung over the rail and collided with the other side of the banister, dangling high above the central room. The flaming ball blazed down the stairs, traveling too fast to stop.

Sterling panted as he braced his boots against the

wall and pushed off. He and Evenna plunged toward the main room's center and its blizzard of black-tipped arrows. His entire body went pale, and his energy withered without his blood magic, yet electricity pulsed through his veins as panic took over. He had leaped into a free fall of at least ten stories with no way to fly or land safely.

He held Evenna tight against his chest and tried to mindspeak with Freya. At the same time, he positioned Evenna's cloak over his head, pulling on the corners for the slightest bit of air resistance. It slowed them greatly. Then, he did what he should not have done. He looked down. In between pockets of blue flame and flying arrows, his reflection stared back at him from the black, glassy floor. His distorted face and oversized eyes seemed to drain of color. The eyes filled with black liquid, and a bloody hand appeared to squeeze his windpipe. He could almost feel the phantom touch of his own blood magic at his throat. Then, his real-life hand slipped. The cloak rippled in the air as they resumed free fall.

His body jolted as hands gripped his shoulder armor. Olive green-and-gold feathers batted the air around him, and his plunge stalled a few stories from the chaotic battle on the floor.

"Nice flying!" Sterling gasped.

"You promised I wouldn't be bored—I'd say you fulfilled your end of the deal," Freya panted. She hissed a warning as a purple apparition burbled into the air—an Elvish ghost soldier.

"There's a balcony," Sterling gestured feebly. "Can you pick up Bance too? We might be able to escape." His arms around Evenna trembled.

"I'm not sure," Freya admitted, but she was already diving for the skeletal warrior. A few powerful strokes took them nearly out of arrow range, but there was a pop, and Freya gasped in pain.

"Sorry—I can't," she heaved, then rolled toward an open hallway only halfway up the wall. The four of them crashed over the handrail, and Freya flopped into a recovery position, inspecting her wing.

Sterling and Bance rose protectively, both shaken but uninjured. But Evenna moaned in pain. Sterling yanked on the remaining purple stub flopping from her wrist. It resisted with great force until he gripped it with his teeth and tugged it out with a squelch like a plump slug. The wound glowed with bright white healing magic as the vine withered. Evenna's sleeping expression calmed.

Sterling hugged her, but his attention was torn. "Freya, are you okay?"

"Fine. I'll be...fine," she whispered, holding her hurt wing. "Might be dislocated," she muttered grimly.

"We can't get out the same way we came in. They would've traced our steps to the kitchen by now," Bance stated the obvious, scanning the corridors around them.

Their time had run out. The fortress was crawling with guards in war mode. The Dark King bellowed from above, and the ghost soldier had just spotted them.

"I think I know a way," Freya groaned, forcing her body upright. "Bance, keep that staff hot—blast a hole in the wall and don't get spooked when I say to jump."

"Are you sure?" Sterling asked, furrowing his sweaty brow, his thoughts sluggish. If only he could find a way to retrieve his blood magic—and his troll dagger. Though, his weapons didn't matter if they couldn't make it out safely.

Bance nodded, patting Sterling's shoulder to reassure him.

"Now, bones!" she commanded, tucking her head beneath puffed feathers and wrapping her wings around Sterling and Evenna.

Blue fire whooshed out of Bance's staff, incinerating the smooth, black stone and searching out weaknesses. When the light dimmed, a shoulder-wide hole had opened into the sky.

CHAPTER TWENTY-SEVEN
BREAKNECK MANEUVERS

On Freya's cue, they jumped from the scraggly exit hole into the frosty howling wind. Sterling's energy was depleted, so he dropped like a sack of pecans with his arms around Evenna. A squawking echoed in his ears, and Freya's plan came to fruition. Two blackbirds dove to catch the tumbling humans on their backs. Sterling had no choice but to trust them. He was too weak to protest —using every ounce of energy to hold himself and Evenna aboard the exceedingly fast bird. It was smaller than a dragon but made up for it with speed. But how long would they be able to keep this pace? He glanced at his shoulder armor and spotted a tiny dragon figure. He chewed his lip and decided not to summon Green—yet. His dragon brother was the key to uniting the dragon clans and the only chance at convincing them to fight against the next wave of dark soldiers. No, Sterling needed to get home another way.

The blackbirds' graceful wings twitched as they gauged the southern current, propelling them away from the fortress and over the sea.

"You did well, feathers," Bance hollered into the pelting wind.

Freya turned and smiled at her backseat passenger, rubbing her wing. "It's strange to be a rider instead of a flyer."

The fresh wind blew in Evenna's face, and she awoke, thrashing.

"Whoa! Stay still. Evenna, it's okay. I've got you. We're going home," Sterling soothed.

"Home?" she asked in genuine confusion, furrowing her dark eyebrows.

"Everen. Don't you remember? Your grandfather, Tomorak?" he prodded.

Her new purple eyes shifted, searching for the truth—her memories. But the intelligent gleam faded as her body went limp again. Bance tilted his shrouded head at the girl.

Instead of calming the farther they flew from the fortress, Sterling's nerves tingled as he crooked his neck.

"What's wrong?" Bance was immediately alert.

"My blood magic found me, but it's being followed," Sterling said, pinpointing three flying objects behind them.

The first object to reach them was merely a flash

of white until Sterling caught its handle, revealing the troll dagger. He scanned for his blood magic, but the closest object crackled with dark flames. The elven king's fireball still hadn't dissipated.

"A parting gift from our friends?" Bance sighed.

"I don't think the king will forgive me for the dagger scar across his face anytime soon," Sterling said matter-of-factly as the fireball gained speed.

"We can try to redirect it into the sea," Freya suggested, eyeing Bance and his bulky figure.

Sterling mustered up the last of his energy. "I'll do it. My bird has the lighter load—we can go faster. If you could explain everything to it," he gestured to his mount.

"Her, not it," Freya clarified and began squawking animatedly at Sterling's mount. The blackbird cawed affirmatively and pulled into a dive. The fireball sparked overhead, then leaned into a graceful curve to give chase. The bird tilted her head, gauging the fire's trajectory. Her wings twitched, pivoting in another direction as her body twirled nearly upside down. Sterling clutched desperately at Evenna's body while clinging to the bird's body with every muscle in his legs. Wing tips skipped across the frigid crests of the sea waves, but the fireball stopped just short of plunging into a watery oblivion. Their plan had failed, and Sterling had nearly lost his grip on Evenna's frail body.

"Tell her to try again!" he shouted to Freya, bear-hugging the witch as he repositioned himself against the bird's back.

Their next attempt to lure the flaming nuisance into the sea had no more success than the first. Trying to outmaneuver it was proving impossible. The bird began to tire, but the fireball showed no signs of wear. Eventually, the blackbird was too fatigued to do more than fly slightly faster than the deadly fire. Sterling was drained too. His pulse throbbed weakly, and he was growing lightheaded. He was failing his new pack. What a disappointment he would be to his village—to his father's name. Then, he remembered something his father had said—the success of a hunt wasn't just a strong leader, it was the strength of the pack working together.

"A storm's coming," Bance shouted as foreboding clouds swept over the deep, blue ocean with alarming speed.

"Bance, do you have any power left in your staff? Freya, I know your wings are injured, but how are your shooting arms?" Sterling called, refusing to give up hope.

The skull-topped staff flickered with a dim blue glow before going dark again, and Bance shook his head. Freya reached for her crossbow and arrow, wincing as the trigger grazed her injured wing.

"I can't hit it—not with my injury," she began to argue.

Sterling signaled toward a low point in the air, and

Bance instinctively held her wing so she had a clear shot.

"Don't worry. We'll do this together," Sterling affirmed.

"Fine. Steady!" She exhaled deeply as the arrow buzzed through the choppy wind.

Sterling assessed the arrow's velocity and trajectory, then leaned his body weight to guide his bird where they needed to go. The fireball pursued. At a precise point in the sky, he pushed one of the bird's wings, intentionally dropping them out of the arrow's range before the fireball could react. When the arrow struck the flaming globe, it exploded, sending sizzling bits of charred fire in every direction. Each glob hissed as it plopped into the cold ocean water. Meanwhile, Sterling's bird was also on a crash course with the sea. Caught in an opposing wind current, she was unable to regain control and dodge the fiery downpour at the same time.

He squeezed Evenna, bracing for impact, but the sensation of saltwater was already burning inside his nostrils and stinging the still-healing flesh of his face. Beneath the rustling ocean, a pounding headache attacked the front of his skull. Childish rumors of sea people with glittering fins crossed his mind before he realized he needed to breathe. Recalibrating, he kicked hard, swimming toward the ocean's surface with Evenna in tow. He gulped the salty air, hoisting her over his shoulders, and into air lit only by flashes of ragged lightning.

"Freya!" he yelled, his voice muted by the crashing waves and roaring wind. "Bance!"

He searched for his friends but instead caught a glimpse of black feathers bobbing then sinking into the ocean. His bird was drowning.

Evenna's cloak, he remembered.

He tucked the fabric around her and spoke to her in her mind. *Evenna, activate your cloak to float above the water. I have to leave you for a moment—Evenna!* He screamed internally, fumbling desperately for her pearl.

When his slippery fingers gripped the magical sphere, her cloak illuminated with a silver glow, hoisting her above the smacking waves. He gulped, filling his lungs with moist air before diving toward the fading glimmer of black feathers. Within seconds, the water pressure was pressing into his eardrums and his ribs felt as though they'd burst. But he was determined not to let the salty abyss take the loyal creature. Grasping one oily wing, he pulled her up and over his head. A branch-like leg thumped against his chest, and his breath whooshed from his lungs in little bubbles that squiggled up out of sight. Flipping upside down, he positioned his boots against the bird's middle and shoved with whatever strength he had left. She drifted toward the surface as his body sank into darkness. As all light faded, the numbing depths of the sea embraced him, and he drifted into a breathless sleep.

CHAPTER TWENTY-EIGHT
THE RED WOLF

Sterling awoke with the warmth of sunlight caressing his shoulders and his face pressed against a bed of red fur. The murmuring of chatter filled his ears as he blinked away salt crystals.

"Well, look who took a beauty nap," Bance teased, looking unscathed and spry in his non-shadow form. His pale green skin looked solid in the crisp light of day, but Sterling's vision blurred as he scanned his surroundings.

"It is good to see you, friend," a husky voice boomed.

Sterling smiled, instantly recognizing the vibrations from the huge body beneath him.

"It's been a long time, Red Wolf. Thank you for coming for us," Sterling began. Judging by the sun's angle and wind direction, the great wolf was walking over the ocean toward Everen, the storm at his back.

"Your spirit friend pulled you from the ocean—

you're lucky. But the Vionin Kingdom is in bad shape. Shadow elves sabotaged the kingdom's entire supply of blood beetle juice, and we've been racing frantically to brew more. The princess agreed I should retrieve you and return promptly. The dark elves will attack again, but the plendi and other respectable magic doers agree there are no signs of dark magic returning this day—we have some time. Green has journeyed to the other dragon clans, hoping to rally as many dragons as possible to stand guard and fight when the time comes. Oh, Freya sent the blackbirds home. It's a shame they belong to the dark elves— good birds," the Red Wolf glanced over his furry shoulder.

"My bird was drowning," Sterling uttered.

"Your bird told me what you did," said Freya from farther up the wolf's back. "That was brave, Sterling, but you nearly died saving one blackbird—who, had I not bribed her with the whereabouts of treats in their storage shed, may not have helped us at all," she scolded. Sterling choked down a gasp. One of her magnificent wings hung at an awkward angle, and her limp feathers were streaked blackish red.

"Freya, your injuries, I'm so sorry."

She shrugged. "Trust me, I've had it worse."

"She can't fly until she sees a healer, but all things considered, it was a successful quest," Bance interjected.

"Bance!" Sterling's head swung around. "I owe you my life. How did you find me?"

"Your bird called to us. When I'm in shadow form, I don't need to breathe. Everyone where I'm from competes in diving tournaments. And you don't owe me anything. Just help our sky Dorien here find a healer and we're even. Are there good healers in Everen?"

Sterling's mind swirled as memories of his homeland rushed back to greet him like the notes of a familiar tune.

"Yes. Evenna's grandfather is our village Alin. He heals magic doers of all sorts, from dragons to...wait, where is Evenna?"

He tried to hold back a panicked expression but couldn't help whirling to look for her. Pain lanced up his neck, and his vision swam as Evenna's slouched form appeared only a few inches behind him. He closed his eyes, then looked down at his hands. They were pale and trembling slightly. His energy was slowly returning, but he worried he'd lost his magic blood for good. He focused his hunter senses, but there was no spike of pain as he'd grown accustomed to. He had lost so much blood in the storm, but it seemed to have taken the cave bug poison with it.

"She woke up earlier and went on about her father needing her—something about her purpose? Strange girl," Freya remarked.

"She said father? Or grandfather?" Sterling demanded.

Freya yawned and laid her head against her good wing. "Does it matter?"

"It might," he whispered.

The Red Wolf's ears twitched. "Sterling Fierce, we will be in Everen soon, and Evenna is safe. Your quest was yet another successful one. You can stop worrying now."

Most of their journey was silent except for the rhythmic splashing of wolf paws against the waves. Although not permanent, his enchantment permitted him to run over water for a time. It wasn't exactly like flying, more like hovering with a bounce, but it got the job done.

Evenna had woken, opening her usual pale silvery-blue eyes and looking much more like herself. She explained that her blood had been tainted, but she thought she could control it with practice. Sterling offered to help teach her. If anyone knew about controlling their blood, he did.

"I knew you missed me," Sterling said with a boyish grin.

"I miss home and soap. You need a bath," Evenna pinched her nose, blushing slightly behind a smile.

"Evenna, what do you remember about the dark elves?" Freya pried, wincing in discomfort as her damaged wing shifted unintentionally.

"I didn't see much," Evenna replied calmly. "The water sprites left me on Zaharen, and I was kept in a room filled with plants—the elves gave me food and drink, like a guest. But then the king started to visit, and he started the…improvements, he called them. He said if I went through with it, I'd be powerful enough to bring my mother back."

The Red Wolf slowed his pace. "We're almost to Everen. There is still dark magic in the air. It's best to stay hidden for now."

Everen's shores appeared from behind the chest-deep wolf fur, and Sterling relaxed slightly. The mountainous Northern Ice Lands, fittingly, were blanketed in snow and ice and gleamed majestic purple in the sunlight. But near the snowy shore, hundreds of ships were docked, all flying black sails and cryptic symbols of knotted thorns and rope. Muddy trails of footprints slithered from the ships to the mountain, right behind the Vionin Kingdom.

Leaping from the ocean to solid land, the Red Wolf skirted the mountains, warily approaching the kingdom. Towers were ablaze, littered with chunks of missing stone. Though the castle stood, it was damaged, stained with telltale purple residue of the ghost soldiers. Silently, the wolf transformed. His fur lightened until colorless, and every muscle became clear as water.

"It reeks of dark magic here," Freya whispered.

"It reeks of death," Bance added.

The Red Wolf sniffed the ground, stirring up feathers both jet-black and cloud-white. "Their fleet has returned, larger than before, but the dark elves are not here," the Red Wolf said.

He carried them to the center of the kingdom before restoring his vibrant, solid form. Sterling caught Evenna's worried expression and gave her a reassuring smile.

"Welcome home," he mouthed.

"Freya, the royal family has healers—tree gnomes and plendi. Sterling can take you to them. Evenna, they can evaluate you and offer light-magic enchantments and cleansing spells," the wolf offered before rushing them off to speak with the Vionin King.

Maybe they can help find my missing blood, Sterling desperately hoped. Without it, he was no witch hunter. If not a witch hunter, he wasn't sure what he was.

CHAPTER TWENTY-NINE

THE QUEEN'S CALL

"This way," Sterling said in a low voice. A red figure flashed in the distance, and Sterling paused to watch as the Red Wolf bent to help clear rubble from the street.

"He's a good friend to you," Bance said.

"He's more than that. He's Everen's protector. We're strong enough to defeat any army as long as he's here," Sterling replied.

Evenna's eyes darted to pockets of amethyst flames sprouting from the towers. She tried to avoid staring at the feathery lumps strewn across the ground.

"Does this lead to the food hall?" Bance squinted at the painted bowl of soup on a torn wooden sign.

"Indeed, or at least what is left of it," the sign remarked in a lilting accent. "We are unsure of the damages, though I would imagine the storage kitchen is untouched if the reinforced stone held up to the fire." A yellow path lit up behind the sign.

Bance rubbed his eyes.

Sterling grinned. "The Vionin Kingdom is a magical place. Its signs and maps all talk. The paths are colored so you don't get lost easily. It looks like the healers are near the palace."

"I'll take the one with food at the end of it." The ghost Dorien's stomach growled as he followed the yellow road.

"Sterling Fierce, is that you?" the sign sniffled. "I'm afraid I have no way to see at present."

"It is me." Sterling glanced around, activating his hunter's sight. Part of the sign was lodged beneath a cracked boulder. He hurriedly retrieved the board and secured it with a bent nail.

"That is indeed kind of you. The princess and her family are in an undisclosed location, unavailable for audiences at the present time, of course," the sign said preemptively.

"Of course. Do you think it'd be okay if my friends met with her plendi?"

"I cannot think of a reason why not. Take the royal road—you know the one," the sign managed a creaky wink.

"This place is different than I could have imagined. Even with the destruction, it's so enchanting," Evenna gasped, taking Sterling's hand. His heart thumped a little faster, but he was careful not to grip her hand too tightly as they proceeded along a violet-colored path.

"The princess's tower is over there. She has plendi —half plant, half fairy. Just do as they say or you'll get an earful," Sterling warned.

"Are they good healers?" Freya huffed, bracing her injured wing with both arms.

Sterling nodded. "They are splendid healers. And Evenna, I'd like them to see you too."

Evenna twisted her face momentarily but didn't protest.

Each step was softly padded by a carpet of lavender moss, and as they climbed toward the highest point in the city, they were surrounded by colorful chimney smoke from cottages that had survived the attack.

"What is happening to the sky?" Freya asked.

"And the ground?" Evenna added.

Tree bark coated the ground where one would expect grass to grow, and the trees were actually thick blades of grass, braided to form trunks and limbs. Dirt and mud leaves sprouted, decorated with twigs and pebbles, while a stream flowed through the sky.

"Like I said. This place was built by magic," Sterling stated, waving them to a medium-sized tower made of stone. Its walls were adorned with golden markings and lined with flower bushes of assorted colors. The ornate door was charred slightly but still the same beautifully flower-covered oval he remembered it to be.

"Welcome to the princess's tower," he announced.

A voice immediately answered his knock. "I told you we'd have a visitor! Berry, come!"

The door swung open, and the bedraggled group was greeted by a tiny flying lady with mint-green skin and eyes sparkling like emeralds.

"Hi, Merry. I'm so glad you're alright," Sterling said, taking in the scent of fresh flowers wafting from inside the tower.

She squealed, and she darted in to hug his neck, her sparkles dripping down his clothing.

"You brought friends?" Berry, a plump curly-haired plendi hovered near the entrance with a playful smile.

The oldest plendi floated toward them, fists on her hips.

"Yes, Berry. Sterling Fierce needs something. That's why he's here—the same for his friends. Merry—enough, you're glittering everywhere," she swatted at a greenish sparkle.

"That's true. We need your help," he admitted. "But I have missed you. Even you, Nael."

"Yes, yes. Let's get to it. The feathered one is obviously wounded and cannot fly unless properly healed. Dear, come with me," Nael motioned to Freya. "You'll need to stay a while—I smell dark magic. Let's hope it isn't already infected."

Freya glanced back at Sterling before stepping inside the princess's tower.

"Well, you two look alright," Berry beamed.

Merry ignored her sister and zipped around to inspect her guests from all sides.

"No, there's something wrong. Sterling Fierce is missing most of his magic. And the girl's blood is in turmoil. Two types inside, but only one can prevail. Terrible business, having to choose which part of you mustn't go on," Merry whispered.

Evenna shot an annoyed look at Sterling, but he shook his head, and she merely scowled.

Berry nibbled on her lip. "What should we do?"

"Take them to the tree gnome, of course. Blood is not our specialty," Merry said calmly.

They clamored up the tower stairs, ducking beneath loose vines and through wisps of miniature butterflies. Merry and Berry led the way, trailing glowing dust in their wake.

"Oh, Sterling Fierce, the battle was dreadful. We helped prepare the healing quarters as the wounded came in. Many magic doers joined the fight but lost their nerve after seeing the dark elves in battle—still in hiding or fled the kingdom, some did. But who can blame them? It was terrifying. The Vionin Army did what it could, but many were lost. We summoned the Lost Guardian Hunters, but they were stranded in the East by a blizzard—the worst one we've had in centuries. If it hadn't been for the Red Wolf, we'd have perished," Berry rattled on animatedly.

"Here we are. Shhh, let's call him now," Merry murmured as she tapped methodically on an unmarked stone wall.

Vivid green light revealed a squatty round door no taller than Sterling's knees. A tree gnome shuffled out, tilting his head up to study his guests. The top of his head was smooth bark, reminding Sterling of a balding old man.

"Hunter, come down here, suppose you do," the tree gnome instructed.

Face to face with the gnome, Sterling tried not to stare at the sausage-shaped wooden nose. The gnome's amber eyes flashed with light inside, then he laughed softly.

"I'm not trying to be funny," Sterling swallowed his own smile. "I've lost my..." He held up his arms helplessly.

"You've found more than you've lost. Yes, suppose so," the gnome said seriously. He turned to Evenna without another word.

Sterling despised when magic doers spoke in riddles, but instead of growing irritable, sorrow flooded his chest. He had his answer. His blood would remain lost, and there was nothing he could do about it.

"Troubling, I suppose so, young witch," the gnome's mood darkened. He hummed a melody with sour notes and creaking sounds. He raised his limbs and seized a glowing teal cylinder from the air over his smooth head.

"Light for you to see two paths. Remember, you chose, nobody else chooses for you. Trust yourself... suppose that you should," he said. He swished his arms, and the light splashed over Evenna, dissipating into a thousand sprinkles. Her skin absorbed the light, and she began to glow. Before she could say anything, the tree gnome was gone, the stone door vanishing with a click.

"What kind of magic was that?" Sterling whispered to Merry.

"Elemental—like the elves use," Merry said as Berry bumped into her.

"Why are we whispering—is it secret?" Berry inched closer, wide-eyed.

"I was just telling Sterling about elemental magic," Merry murmured.

"Oh, the old laws? Boring ol' dusty texts if you ask me. Too many rules," Berry spouted.

"What can you tell me about them?" Sterling asked with one arched eyebrow.

"Well, deary," Berry began, "the ancient laws of the elements are all written down in books protected by the strongest Elvish magic. Let's see, did Elvish law come first, or was it the pure elements? Anyway, there's fire, water, and sky. Oh, rock—it's the neutral one, easy to forget."

Sterling and Evenna thanked the plendi sisters, then followed the path to the food hall. They found the cooking area nearly empty, but the portly kitchen sprites had outfitted Bance with an apron, and he was dutifully frying potato cakes in a skillet. A snuffling came from outside.

"There you are!" The Red Wolf sat outside the

kitchen. "The Elvish Queen has called. The Pearl Castle is under attack. We must go now—we may already be too late," the Red Wolf panted.

Bance hurriedly wrapped the potato cakes in his apron, and the three climbed aboard the Red Wolf's back. Soon they were bounding over the Vionin Kingdom roads and through the nearby woods.

They reached the Hills of Bryght before sundown. The lavender-soiled hills were beaten with fiery craters, and black sludge drenched the once-majestic landscape. Large, thorned balls of twisted vines were strewn about, and their meaty spikes punctured the Pearl Castle. The domed ceilings were split with gaping holes, and the walls cracked. Despair filled Sterling's veins where his magic used to be. But he unsheathed his daggers nevertheless.

CHAPTER THIRTY
A RACE OF BLADES

Through the billowing smoke, elves sliced at each other with swords nearly as tall as their wielders. Illuminated blades sparked, and metal clanged against metal. Overhead, winged creatures dove in timed attacks, releasing high-pitched screeches in the late evening air. Well-aimed spears of pure Elvish steel zipped through the skies, making a disturbing *thunk* as they punctured their targets. Everenian ivory cloaks whirled as their wearers battled dark-hooded enemies. As savage and chaotic as the scene was, watching the elves in combat was like watching an ancient, graceful, and precise form of war. But the Everenian elves were few, and the dark elves, many.

The Red Wolf set the trio at the outskirts of the forest and raced toward the heart of the Pearl Castle to protect the queen. He was immediately set upon by a pair of dark elves, but with a mere flick of his tail and clash of his jaws, his path was open once more.

"Stay hidden and fight only when you have to—save your power for when it's important," Sterling instructed Evenna.

He drew his daggers. Evenna stood rigid, staring at the turmoil.

"Evenna, hide!" he hissed.

Her eyes swirled with a darkness that turned his stomach to ice. His gut unclenched when she squeezed her eyes, shaking the darkness loose. She gave a weak smile, then turned to tiptoe between the mud-splattered bushes.

Bance raised his staff, and the two stood back to back, surveying the threats on the ground and the deadly warriors of the sky. Sterling suddenly wished he'd allowed Barath to persuade him to bring a shield as an Acreedian dragon plummeted from the sky, burning feathers dropping like rain. The majestic creature crashed at his feet, never to fly again. Its turquoise fur was ablaze, and a solitary black arrow was lodged deep in its neck. One wild eye shot open, filled with agony as it gurgled from the fatal wound.

"What is it?!" Bance demanded.

"Cover me," Sterling said, dropping to his knees at the creature's head.

He whispered a hunter's prayer and turned the arrow, guiding it swiftly to stop the creature's suffering. The pair of Acreedian feather symbols on his wrists glowed while he stood guard. A pale blue mist rose from the dragon, and a sphere of light grew around its lifeless body, stretching over Sterling. Bance took a step back and waited for enemies to appear.

For a moment, the war cries and injured screams continued as usual. Then, crunching hoofbeats approached.

"Hunter Sterling, we have our first opponent," Bance warned, crouching with his staff, eyes full of deep-blue fire. He positioned himself opposite Sterling as they both prepared their weapons.

The horse galloped at full speed toward them, its black silk caparison fluttering over its massive body. The rider, a dark elf with luminous silver eyes and thick dragon-scale armor, had the advantage of speed and height. His weapon, a ball with spikes, swung in the air from its chain, releasing an eerie screech as it spun in a perfect circle. The horse sped, aiming for the tiny space between Sterling and Bance.

"Now!" Sterling shouted. They both jumped backward with enough space between them that their attacker was forced to choose one target.

The horse lost no speed, veering toward Bance. There was a crack as the mace glanced off his horned shoulder armor, cracking the plate but barely damaging the Elvish weapon.

"Watch out!" Bance hollered, clutching his shoulder.

Sterling ducked and then rolled out of the ball's path. From this vantage point, he had a front-seat view of the horse's ragged feet. Black goo seeped through the cracked hooves, hinting at the aggressive enchantments upon the animal. Sterling squirmed away from the nightmarish legs and rolled to his feet to avoid the mace once again. The spiked ball whipped around again, and Sterling only had enough time to cross his daggers above his head to absorb the impact. Wherever the Elvish weapon touched the troll dagger, its metal spikes melted into vapor. Hope rose in Sterling's chest, and he slashed determinedly, hacking at the mace.

"This troll stuff really works," Sterling said, relieved and impressed.

"You think you're clever, but you're not," the hooded rider stated.

He increased his speed, flailing the jagged ball until it was all Sterling could do to dodge. His loss of blood became apparent again, and Sterling strained to keep his arms steady. He had underestimated the dark elf's strength and wished he were up against a dozen fog soldiers instead. Sterling slid backward inch by inch, unable to match the brute force of his opponent but refusing to surrender. Suddenly, Bance barreled into the mix, colliding with the horse. A terrible bray came from the stallion as it transformed to black goo and splattered in all directions. The dark elf suddenly found himself falling into a puddle of muck, but he pulled himself up gracefully, grumbling in his native Elvish language, a chilling mix of whispers and grunts.

Even without his mount, the elf's stature was imposing. Sterling took a hunter's attack pose, inviting the elf to fight him. The dark elf tossed his mangled mace into the black goo and drew a gleaming silver sword.

"I commend your warrior's spirit. But it won't save you or your friends," he said.

The weighty sword slashed at Sterling's middle, and he jumped back, taking advantage of his hunter agility. But the elf never slowed. Striking in quick succession, the blade sliced Sterling's cape as he ducked and weaved. Sterling's movements grew more labored, driving home the reality of fighting an immortal. Sterling could dodge the elf's attacks, but not for much longer. He scanned the area for his friends. Bance lay on the ground, stunned from head-butting the muscular horse, his staff quivering in the dim light. Behind him, Evenna crouched behind a pile of scorched branches peppered with pockets of purple fire. Her eyes were wide in horror.

An overwhelming desire spread in his veins to avenge the pain and fear the dark elves had brought upon his homeland. Instead of trying to elude his attacker, this time, he lunged forward, his family dagger first. Green-and-red flame entwined along its blade. He sliced upward, then thrust his troll-tooth dagger into the dark elf's face. The thick fabric of the elf's hood withered upon contact, and the tattered hood slid away to reveal a brooding stare. The dark elf wasted no time in retaliating, and Sterling leaped back as the huge sword nearly sliced his ankles. He clambered up a pile of thorny remains and flipped backward over his enemy, troll dagger ready. It slashed through the elf's armor, and the black metal disintegrated.

He was forced to dodge back as the elf whirled, blade flashing.

"Very good. But you've chosen the wrong side, Hunter. You are a suitable battle opponent, but it's time to die. All mortals leave this world one way or another. It is your destiny."

The next strike would have pierced Sterling's throat, but the elven blade clattered against something, and Sterling was able to dodge. He rolled across the burnt soil to take cover beneath a discarded kingdom shield. The dark elf frowned at a cork now impaled on his sword while Sterling watched the last of the teleportation potion drip from his neck. Then the shield was bearing down on him, the elf pinning him to the ground underneath it. His cape pulled snug around his neck as Elvish steel pierced the shield and stung his chest. He cringed, but the pressure stopped abruptly as white light erupted near his stomach. His hunter's dagger roared with white flame, and Sterling cast the shield aside. The dark elf was drawing his sword back for a deadly swing, but Sterling knocked it out of the elf's hand with his flaming weapon and jabbed at the elf's feet with the curled tip of his troll dagger.

The dark elf didn't flinch. Instead, he slid his

second sword from its waist. He raised it slowly, taking aim as if performing an execution. Still pinned on his back and brutally fatigued, Sterling gripped his daggers and prayed for an escape from the fatal blow. He scanned the elf's plated chest, searching for a hunter's mark. Miraculously, it appeared, and he aimed, hurling the flaming dagger in the air while the elf's sword plunged down. It was a race of the blades.

The elf growled, clutching the dagger as fire spread to his arms, chest, and neck. His blade pounded against the charred soil, proving that while he was stronger, Sterling was faster. Time slowed as Sterling scrambled to his feet, watching the elf drop to the ground. His robed body writhed disturbingly before melting into a dark purple liquid, oily and smelling of burnt hair.

"Is he dead?" Evenna called, from her hiding spot, fingertips aglow with white light.

"I don't know," Sterling said, trying to catch his breath.

"If that's what happens to elves, then that ocean of white puddles means our friends have been liquefied, too many to count," she said.

"Try not to think about it right now. Thanks for your help, Evenna—I couldn't have done it without you and Bance. Ghost, you okay?" He breathed heavily, scanning the area for more dark soldiers.

"Elves are immortal," Bance groaned. He leaned heavily on his staff as he pulled his muscular body upright and assessed his injuries—a gash across his head and a fractured shoulder. "But they can lose their form for a few hundred years—not long enough to forgive you or me or fire fingers over there," he added, smiling at Evenna.

"I want to help," she said proudly, searching Bance and Sterling's eyes for acceptance.

Sterling walked over and squeezed her tightly, tucking her head beneath his chin. He kissed her forehead as a mix of emotions coursed through him, too strong to deny.

And he didn't care if Bance saw.

CHAPTER THIRTY-ONE
ANCIENT LAWS

A white-robed Elvish figure riding an Acreedian dragon zoomed overhead. The dragon's wild cream-colored eyes scanned them. Its milky white feathers were charred and bloodstained. Sterling saluted, and the Elvish soldier placed his fist against his chest and bowed his head as he darted higher into the sky. Evenna whispered something in Sterling's ear.

"Where?"

She pointed north of the castle where a green dragon dipped from the clouds, carrying the Alin and Uncle Roag. The potion wizard soared alongside, using his enchanted staff. A wave of blood beetle bombs rained down in their wake, drenching the dark elves. Some failed to understand the repercussions and continued pouring dark magic onto the battlefield. They quickly regretted it as their own attacks beamed back in their faces. Shadow elves disappeared at the merest touch of the blue juice.

The Red Wolf, with Queen Clarelle on his back, pounced amid a whoosh of scarlet-hued magic. Dark and light elves stopped fighting at the sight.

"I am a protector of Everen and servant to the honorable Queen Clarelle," the Red Wolf announced, eyes blazing like a magical fire against the smoky air.

The queen spoke next. "Dark elves of Zaharen, Army of Eliad, you brought war to our homeland. You are banished from Everen. If you leave now, you may take your lives with you. If you do not, you forfeit my offer indefinitely."

A purple fog rose in a single column, tearing through the red dust and reaching the clouds. It spread slightly at the top, forming a throne where the Dark King sat.

"I have the right to rule this land. The same royal blood in your veins runs in mine, sister!" he exclaimed.

"For centuries, this land has gone through war and peace, but the humans have won the right to rule Everen. I am queen of the Pearl Castle, decreed by the Vionin King himself. You've no right to challenge his decision," the queen returned.

Eliad cackled. "You know mortals are insignificant. Our laws, the elemental laws, allow a challenge to the throne every thousand years, and the time has come for the dark elves to step out of the shadows.

This is Elvish code, or have you forgotten the laws of our ancestors?"

"The laws are clearly written, but they are from a distant past," Queen Clarelle retorted. "Your interpretation of them is far from the intentions of our foremothers and forefathers."

"Laws are laws, I'm afraid," Eliad snorted.

"What if your laws were destroyed?" a small voice rang out.

The Dark King twitched, scanning the crowd with a scowl. "Who interferes?"

"Sterling Fierce, your darkness." He waved his troll dagger. "I'm just wondering, with all your army's fire and destruction, how could your ancient texts possibly have survived? If they were demolished, then I'd assume the laws would be, well, insignificant."

Queen Clarelle spoke. "Hunter Fierce has a point —if your soldiers have indeed burned our texts of Elvish history...along with most of our castle, well, they will be nothing more than charred bits of paper smeared across the castle floors."

"You would have no right to challenge the throne, Eliad of Ohann, and no right to be here," the Red Wolf flicked his tongue over the pointy ends of his yellowed teeth.

The Dark King's pillar of smoke thinned, and he sank slowly.

"You have incited war upon Everen elves, which means you have chosen war with all Everen. You will never be king here!" the queen declared.

"Everen fights together!" Green hollered. A hoard of dragons flooded in overhead, drowning the glow of the stars.

Sterling smiled, inhaling the refreshing sensation of hope.

The potion wizard summoned a wave of blood beetle juice that crested higher than the castle walls then crashed upon the battlefield. In its wake, a whole battalion of night trolls raged into the mud, a nearly unstoppable force once the dark magic had been subdued by blood beetles. The Troll Queen and her son looked larger and more terrifying than before, adorned with battle tattoos and spiked bone armor. Suddenly, the dark elves had lost their greatest advantages.

With the soldiers occupied in battle, Sterling, Bance, and Evenna dodged toward the fizzling smoke pillar where they'd last seen the Dark King. A trail of purple wisps led them to a gaping hole in the castle's wall. The palace itself was in chaos. Ceilings were broken, ancient trees were on fire, and many of the light fixtures had been put out or broken.

"Which way did he go?" Bance asked, slipping in and out of shadow form. Blood still trickled from the wound on his head, but he ignored it.

Sterling pointed to the top of a staircase.

"You can track him because of his dark magic?" Evenna asked, wide-eyed.

"There's purple residue from the fog he was floating on. It's on the steps." He smiled.

"Oh."

Bance walked in between the pair, murmuring in troll dialect.

"What's your problem?" Sterling hissed.

"You two are distracting each other. If you don't focus on the threat, you'll both end up dead." He took a shuddering breath and leaned heavily on his staff before pushing on. Sterling and Evenna followed uncomfortably. They reached the bottom of the stairs and found themselves in a maze of pearl-walled tunnels.

"We're lost," Evenna whispered to Sterling after they lost sight of the purple residue yet again.

He shrugged his shoulders, then glanced at Bance, waiting for another reprimand.

Bance huffed. His skin gradually reformed until he appeared mostly human. "Hunter Fierce, if you are the superior tracker, you lead."

Glowing shards crunched beneath Sterling's boots as he stepped forward.

"Listen," he said, stretching his hand toward a shadowed wall.

Evenna turned toward the noise. "Something is sniffing around."

Bance crouched and cocked his head. "Probably a castle rat or lost pet scared from all the commotion," he decided.

"No, it's something else," Sterling whispered. "I know this creature's scent." A shiver tapped against his spine as his eyes landed on the distinct claw marks.

"Whatever you do, stay perfectly still," he warned as a ball of reddish-brown fur came at them, teeth first.

CHAPTER THIRTY-TWO
THE SEEKER

Sterling shoved the creature aside before its vicious jaws could touch Evenna, and it tumbled clumsily to the floor. The bewitched animal, a peculiar mix of fox and bobcat parts equipped with rabbit hind legs and thick, miniature wings, would have been downright adorable if not for its ferocious temperament and the shiny black saliva spilling over its serrated fangs.

Evenna shrieked and twirled away, her cloak making a graceful arc in the air. The creature's mismatched eyes fixed on it in fascination.

"Evenna, give me your cloak!" Sterling said, already reaching for the fabric as the creature rose onto its hind legs. Evenna unbuckled the clasp and backed away. Sterling waved the material in a mesmerizing pattern that seemed to utterly transfix the winged fox-cat-rabbit. It pounced with an almost playful bark, but its huge talons still made gashes in the pearl floor. Oily sickness puddled in its mouth and dribbled past its oversized teeth. It was obviously a witch's creation. Rust-colored fur had fallen out in clumps, and bare patches revealed its ribs jetting out under paper-thin skin. It hadn't eaten or slept in weeks—searching relentlessly for the scent of Evenna and nothing else.

"Distract it, and I'll kill it," Bance said, making an effort to raise his staff despite his drooping shoulder.

Sterling's eyes widened. "No, it's bewitched—it's hunting Evenna and might have information about the elder witches. And I need to know why they stole my book."

"Book?" Bance huffed.

"I can't explain now. Bance, what do you have to eat?" Sterling asked, luring the creature across the room with the dancing cloak.

"Why?"

"I have an idea. Just toss me something. Cheese, meat, anything—hurry!"

Bance mumbled in his native language and fumbled through a leather pouch attached to his belt —the frilly apron had disappeared sometime along their journey.

The creature sniffed the air, torn between Evenna's scent on the cloak and whatever snacks Bance had tucked away. Bance flung a half-eaten potato cake toward Sterling.

He snatched the food out of the air and dropped the cloak to the floor. When the creature sprang forward, Sterling slipped his free hand around its neck, strategically holding the nourishing lump near its snout but not close enough to eat. The seeker struggled to free itself, then went limp. It looked into Sterling's eyes, begging for an end to its misery. When he released the potato cake into its mouth, for a moment, the black drool lessened, and it smacked its mouth like any ordinary animal.

"There's been too much death. I don't want any more innocent life wasted," Sterling said.

You've eased her suffering. Thank you, Sterling. Evenna shed black-purple tears that fizzled into dark smoke as they trickled down her cheek. She smiled sweetly.

"Innocent? That thing'll rip your throat out given the chance," Bance sighed.

Evenna's smile disappeared. "My elders forged her —I've seen them do this before. She's bewitched to hunt her target. She will come for me again when she's not distracted."

Bance rolled his eyes. "I don't enjoy being right about these things, but it's kill or be killed—this is war. Meanwhile, the Dark King is here somewhere doing who knows what—probably about to unleash some diabolical secret weapon or, worse, escape. Come on, we don't have time."

Suddenly, the halls rumbled with a low humming. Sterling's Acreedian dragon feather tattoos gleamed, bathing his skin in pale white-blue light.

"No more innocent lives will come to harm—not on my quest," he commanded.

Bance pushed his cracked shoulder armor together, blinked hard, and firmly grasped his staff. Blue fire zinged out, and Sterling jumped back, but instead of incinerating the seeker, the flames formed a floating sphere around it.

"You are the quest leader, Hunter Sterling. I will hold the creature here—it will not leave my sight. But you will have to fight the Dark King alone," he bowed respectfully, then sagged onto a nearby crate.

Sterling thanked him and grabbed Evenna's hand.

"We'll fight him together," he retorted quietly, smiling at Evenna. Together, they dashed down the darkened hall.

Evenna reclasped her cloak around her neck, hovering over the pearl floors every few steps to keep pace with his hunter's sprint. Sterling used his enhanced sight and tracking abilities, steering them into a dark outdoor space lined with training targets. Racks of colorful weapons lined the walls.

What is this place? Evenna whispered in his mind.

It's a training ground—and a practice arena. Hide up here. Sterling motioning for her to climb a rope ladder at the edge of the room. He crept toward the arena's center alone, careful not to make a sound as he aimed his troll dagger at a tall, slender shadow. He'd noticed the silhouette the second they'd arrived, and he'd recognized it when it twitched at the same moment Evenna mindspoke.

"Your tracking skills are impressive," Eliad said calmly. "Tell me, what kind of hunter are you, Sterling Fierce?"

"Evenna already knows what I am, and she's not afraid of me—I didn't have to trick her or shove dark magic into her veins. We chose not to be enemies—we chose to trust each other."

One more step and then—the shadow withered.

"Things are never that simple, boy." The king's voice took on a singsong quality and rose in pitch. "I used to trust people, but then I was cast into the darkness by my own family. With great power comes greed, never the one without the other, eventually. It's been long enough. I am fighting for my power back—and my daughter."

Sterling cringed at the elf's voice, which now resembled a cat's yowl. But his breath caught, and he blurted his realization.

"You need her power to win the war. If you win, then what? You'd rule a land that doesn't choose you. Times have changed, and people deserve to make their own choices, choose their leaders—you don't get to decide for them," Sterling lectured, buying time. He drew his family dagger and checked the reflection in his blade, spotting Evenna balancing across a trio of wooden beams overhead.

"Evenna," the king drawled, "I know you're here." When he stepped from the shadows, Sterling's eye was immediately drawn to the horrendous gash on his cheek. His flesh had melted down to the bone, and his face was sunken around it. Sterling smiled grimly at the green tendrils of cave bug venom that curled out like an unexpected tattoo. Around the injury, smoky symbols were swirling hypnotically. The king's thin lips curled into a smirk when Evenna sighed.

"I'm sorry. I don't know how to control it, Sterling." Evenna's nostrils flared, and spindly dark purple markings crept over her skin as her eyes darkened until they resembled pure black glass. Her silvery cape transformed into thousands of midnight blue feathers, and she gasped as it carried her to the floor. She stood rigid and silent beside her father.

"Evenna," Sterling called desperately, "all you have to do is ask it to—"

But the two vanished in a whirl of plum smoke. An odor like burnt fruit lingered in their absence, and a resonating wolf howl echoed against the crumbling castle walls.

CHAPTER THIRTY-THREE
CHOICES

S terling followed his instincts back to the
battlefield but stopped as the chaos inter-
cepted him. An Everenian elf and a troll stood
back to back, fighting a group of enchanted dark
horses. Sterling ducked through their swinging blades
and nearly crashed into a cave insect as it trundled
past like a misshapen, multilegged pony. Sterling
raced over a hill and ducked to avoid a fleeing blackbird and a pack of pursuing Acreedian dragons. He
searched frantically for Evenna but was instead met
with a splash of blood beetle juice. He spat and turned
just in time to see a dark elf's shocked expression
when her own spell rebounded, melting her on the
spot. Flames burst overhead as Fire Dragons rounded
up a group of flying dark elves.

Sterling's heart swelled to see the true cohesion of
the Everen elves, night trolls, and dragons—with
other magic doers like the Alin sprinkled in among a

few brave humans, like Uncle Roag. His spirits sank when a huge shadow emerged, teeth bared, to face a lone figure in a light purple cloak. Sterling focused his vision on the Red Wolf standing in front of Queen Clarelle, unwavering, as Evenna's hand stretched toward the great creature. Her movements were stiff, as if she were a marionette. Sure enough, the Dark King stood a safe distance from the confrontation, twirling his fingers like a puppet master. Crimson fur waved in the wind, but Everen's protector refused to attack her, but he turned to the queen—a young troll leaped in front of Sterling, hacking with a vicious barbed ax, blocking the view. Sterling gritted his teeth and barreled up the hill's steep incline, dodging debris and war casualties. When he heaved himself over the hilltop, the queen was nowhere to be seen, and the Red Wolf lay on his side, bleeding from a jagged wound beneath his magical fur. The wolf's stomach quivered, and his breathing was shallow.

Evenna collapsed to her knees, char marks on her fingertips.

"No!" Every vein in his body throbbed.

"I'm afraid you were right, Hunter." The Dark King emerged from the shadows, purple smoke curling around him. "Evenna would not have chosen this, but nonetheless, there are ways to make things happen." Eliad smiled, eyes twinkling.

Sterling approached her slowly, boots inching across the lavender soil.

"Evenna?"

When she opened her eyes, black and pale blue were clashing in them, neither color strong enough to take control. Rasping breaths pounded in Sterling's ears, and he raced to the wolf.

"I'm so sorry," he said, tears burning hot in his eyes.

"There is nothing to be sorry for," the Red Wolf wheezed. "You are a good hunter, Sterling Fierce. And a good friend. Keep Everen safe for me." The golden light in his eyes flickered like lantern fire, then dimmed, like flame being blown away in the night.

"This wasn't supposed to happen!" Sterling screamed, slamming his fists into the ground. The earth cracked as he stormed toward the Dark King, yanking his troll dagger from his belt. Glowing gray tears streamed down his cheeks as he heaved the dagger—which paused in midair.

"Wait!" Evenna shrieked. Sterling was frozen in a beam of white light.

The Dark King smiled. "See what you are capable of, my dear? My sister's forces will crumble at the loss of their heroic wolf. Take care of the boy next, hurry! It's not too late to win the war and secure your fate as the most powerful witch."

"Don't listen to him, Evenna!" Sterling gasped. Her gaze bounced between her father and her friend, and indecision swirled in her eyes.

Sterling took a deep breath. "You don't have to listen to me, either. I was wrong. I didn't trust you to make decisions for yourself. I'm sorry. You have to find the truth within yourself—decide what is right, not just do what others tell you. From now on, I only want to be a guide, not someone giving you demands. I thought you were too inexperienced, but now I know that friends have to trust each other." He smiled as much as the white light allowed.

Blackened tears trickled down Evenna's cheeks, and she closed her eyes. When she opened them, the black had nearly retreated.

"I never wanted to be a powerful witch, but if that is what I am, I will not be one who harms those I love. You may be my blood, but you are not my family." The troll dagger whirled in her light beam, and a swirl of purple appeared in Evenna's other hand. She brought her hands together, and both lights streamed toward the Dark King, releasing Sterling. Eliad conjured a shield just in time to stop the attack, but the troll dagger sliced right through his magic and buried itself in his shoulder. With a cry, he tore it from his flesh and flung it away. Evenna caught it in another beam of light.

"Sterling, you'll need this," she said. Black tear stains smeared her apple-round cheeks, but her eyes were full of determination as she conjured a glowing purple shield for him.

A gentle wave of light washed over them, and Sterling sensed the queen's sorrow at the death of the Red Wolf. The battlefield grew silent as Elvish soldiers lowered their hoods and kneeled. Every living thing looked to the hill where the great wolf had fallen, but solemnity shifted to fury as the Dark King peeked out from behind his shield. Like scattered beads of water joining together, all types of Everen defenders charged the Dark King.

Eliad's head swiveled frantically, then he disappeared into a puff of purple smoke.

"Sterling, go!" Evenna cried.

In full sprint, he pursued the trail of plum flecks that only a hunter could detect. Boots thundered against the hillside behind him, but Sterling was quicker and quieter. Despite the zealous manhunt, he alone tracked a slinking purple shadow to the mouth of a small cave.

"Eliad, there's nowhere to run. Your plan failed— yes, the Red Wolf was a symbol of strength. But his death will be an everlasting symbol of unity," Sterling said.

The shadow faded, then reformed as the Dark King faced him. Green eyes glowed beneath his hood, and his dagger wound dripped steadily.

"Each failure eliminates one possibility, but there are other possibilities. The dark world has decreed it is not my time, but there will be one chosen—one destined to rule." A thorny vine whipped out of the shadows. Sterling instinctively jabbed at it with Evenna's shield. Blue shimmered on its surface, and the dark magic rebounded, coiling around Eliad's chest, pinning his arms to his body.

"Power is a responsibility earned by friendship

and trust, and no one is destined to rule over another," Sterling raised his throwing hand.

"Do what you've come to do, witch hunter. But I will haunt you and your children. And their children —" he gurgled as the troll blade sank deep into his chest.

The Dark King's body slowly imploded, then melted to dark sludge that withered the meadow grass. Sterling's dagger made a hefty thud against the ground as the Dark King vanished.

Within the hour, Queen Clarelle and her warriors had encircled the site, chanting in Elvish. Sterling found Evenna still atop the hill, kneeling beside the Red Wolf. Sterling touched the wolf's forehead and recited a hunter's prayer.

"I am sorry, Sterling. I would do anything to bring him back," she said softly.

Sterling extended his open hand to her. "Me too."

"I guess *he's* gone too," she said, gulping as Sterling's bloodstained dagger caught her attention.

Sterling nodded. "I'm sorry too, Evenna. I know you wanted to find your family—your true home."

"Maybe I already found it. I just didn't see," she whispered, wrapping her arms around him.

Sterling shut his eyes to the battlefield, the loss of blood in his fingers, and the bursts of magic in the distance. He just held her.

CHAPTER THIRTY-FOUR
GIFTS

The war was over, but there was still much to be done. Elves scoured the battlefield for injured comrades and secured the pearly remains of fallen elves in special containers to await their restoration. Most were carefully stored in hollow jewelry, beads, or sculpted crystals where the warriors could rest until they were ready to re-form after a few hundred years. A workshop had been cleared inside the castle for the laborious task of cleansing and ensuring each flask was complete.

Queen Clarelle not only enchanted containers, she also performed healing for any who were injured. Sterling waited as Uncle Roag, his Alin, and the potion wizard all received gifts of healing and Elvish enchantments along with the gratitude of a great nation. The queen's skin glowed with warm healing light, summoning power from across her kingdom, as she recited prayers over each visitor in her ancient language. She waved her fingers over torn night troll flesh and broken dragon scales, healing them and reversing dark magic infections. When Sterling's turn came, he bowed and presented her with a single strand of the Red Wolf's fur.

"Queen Clarelle, can you bring him back to us?" he begged.

"I am deeply saddened at the loss of our great Red Wolf, but his death is beyond Elvish magic. I'm sorry, Sterling Fierce." Her eyes were kind but sorrowful. "Yet I have a gift for you, a companion who will carry you swiftly when you are in need. This is in gratitude for your alliance in the Battle of the Elves." She bowed her head, and an Acreedian dragon stepped forward. "She is brave, like you. Calla, her name translates to 'restless one.' It is a suitable pairing."

Sterling wiped at his cheeks and stepped back to admire the majestic creature.

"Thank you for such an honor. I do have one other request," he said, hoping to sound as respectable as his father. His Acreedian dragon feather tattoos glimmered. Calla shuffled her wings and bowed. The tips of her wings pulsed electric teal as she stood next to him.

The queen nodded with understanding. "The Troll Queen and I have come to an agreement. It will take time, but their curse can be broken."

Sterling exhaled until he chuckled in his belly, relieved that the trolls would have no reason to dishonor him—and bite his head off.

Bance appeared across the crowded quarters, and the queen gestured for him to approach. He was in daylight form and glanced down nervously. He swayed on his feet, leaning on his staff for balance. The crowd parted to allow the blazing sphere through after him. Its surface was worn, and the seeker had nibbled a small hole in it. The bewitched creature sniffed through the opening, catching Evenna's scent. It flailed its claws in her direction.

"Why did he bring that here?" Evenna squeaked into Sterling's ear.

"I think Bance knows something we don't—and I still want to know why it stole my book," Sterling whispered.

"Queen, this creature was conjured with witch's magic—light witches, from what I understand. Can her bewitchment be lifted and her spirit saved?" Bance asked, lifting his chin.

"It is certainly not ordinary or practiced magic in this land." The queen's piercing eyes seemed to read Bance's soul. "You call yourself a ghost Dorien, but underneath, you are much more. As you are a friend of Sterling Fierce, I will heal your battle damages and grant you this gift. However, by the next blue moon, you must tell him your secret." She arched a silvery eyebrow.

Bance stared warmly at the oddly shaped creature. She gnawed at the hole in her container, slathering black saliva against its curved confinement. "I agree," he said.

"Very well," she said, winking at Sterling.

Evenna elbowed Sterling's ribs as something in his chest pocket stirred. The pearl she'd made popped out and floated into the queen's hand. Queen Clarelle whispered an Elvish spell, absorbing the witches' magic from the seeker into the pearl. The creature moaned and thrashed, but abruptly, it fell still. It licked its lips, clearing away the black froth. Sparks flew, and a pillar of light shone from the creature until it let out a howl, bursting from its protection bubble.

"She's free now," the queen whispered.

Bance scooped up the knee-high creature, then whispered in its ear. It stretched its tiny wings and yawned, scanning the crowd before pouncing toward Evenna. She flinched away, but the seeker merely licked her hand.

"I figured she'd be a good guardian for you, Evenna. I'm sorry I doubted your intentions before. Please keep her," Bance said, bowing his head.

"That's very thoughtful," she stuttered, "but I can't...I don't deserve a gift at all. It's my fault the Red Wolf—"

Queen Clarelle interrupted, "Our princess, created of both light and dark magic, you have chosen to stand against darkness. The death of the great wolf was not your choice."

Evenna avoided eye contact with the seeker but stroked her furry head calmly as Queen Clarelle sent the pearl floating back to Sterling.

"The answers you seek are inside the pearl. In time, you will hear its voice. If you decide to listen to it, you will learn more than the whereabouts of your blood magic and your book, but it may be more than you bargained for," she warned.

A nervous smile warmed his face, but he took the pearl gingerly nonetheless.

When it was clear they would do more good at home than in the elven lands, the Alin and Uncle Roag rode off toward Bren. Bance wished to reunite with Freya, and he and the potion wizard set off along the road to the Vionin Kingdom. Green invited Sterling and Evenna to his emerald castle, and soon the two had mounted Calla, Evenna clutching the seeker on her lap while Sterling kept his arms around them both during the long flight.

"I'm still unsure about the name, Astiana," Evenna admitted.

"Then why'd you name her that?" Sterling replied.

Evenna shrugged. "I don't know. Maybe it's the name she asked for."

"Well, if she asks for anything else, tell her to take a nap. It's going to be a long flight."

"But a warm welcome!" Green insisted.

Sterling closed his eyes, embracing the cold clouds swishing across his face.

"Well, the dragons aren't all united, so perhaps not as warm as we could hope," Green mused.

"You worry too much. Besides, after a battle with immortals, how hard could it be to get a few thousand dragons to be nice?" Sterling asked confidently.

"We'll need all the luck we can get," Evenna said, wrapping her slippers around Sterling's boots. He tucked his head against Evenna's velvety cloak and let the events over the past few days drift away.

They flew over Everen by starlight, and Astiana let out a howl that echoed through the crisp night air.

"Whatever comes next, we face it together," Sterling whispered.

IF YOU LIKE THIS, YOU MAY ALSO ENJOY: MORE THAN LIFE
MORE THAN LIFE BOOK ONE BY BETHANIE FINGER

A gripping story of overcoming grief, self-realization, and embarking on the adventure of a lifetime.

As the daughter of a high-ranking sea captain, nineteen-year-old Cordelia Kimbal lives a life of luxury in the sea faring kingdom of Mikiria. But when her father dies unexpectedly, she is stripped of her title and home, and forced to join the working class in order to survive.

Determined to rise above her losses, Cordelia is eager to prove her worth and stand on her own. But four months after her father's passing, a mysterious letter arrives containing the secret location of the mythical island of Qualaris. Known for concealing the secrets of magic and eternal life, Qualaris is often dismissed as mere legend, but Jasper, Cordelia's father's enigmatic apprentice, is convinced of its existence and is harboring its secrets— secrets that the dark enchanter, Janus would stop at nothing to obtain.

For generations, Jaspar and his ancestors have pursued the discovery and rescue of Qualaris while battling a curse of nonexistence, and he believes that Cordelia is the island's true protector, the only one who can save it and its people from Janus's impending threat.

Faced with the daunting task of defending Qualaris and its people, Cordelia embarks on a quest to locate the island, embrace her birthright, and take on the darkest enchanter in history. If she doesn't, the island and its people won't be the only casualties of Janus's war.

ACKNOWLEDGMENTS

I owe a hefty gratitude to early readers, supportive friends and family, and encouraging passersby. Thank you, Sirah J., for sprinkling your editing magic once again. My heartfelt appreciation goes to you--to Everen's stars and back.

A wholehearted thanks to David Beers for your spirited encouragement and support, always and without fail. To Wise Wolf Books and each staff member I've had the pleasure of working with during this experience, I am forever grateful for your esteemed professionalism and kindness.

To my husband, James, thank you for gifting me countless evenings to vanish from this world and instead, take flight in Everen and beyond.

Lastly, to our dog, Archie. May you enjoy snoring at my feet for many more books to come.

ABOUT THE AUTHOR

Lori Tchen was born and raised in the Texas hill country where shaking out one's shoes for scorpions was part of the daily norm. She writes fiction in the evenings, her highly prized downtime outside of work, while raising her two sons.

Lori's career began in criminology, working deep nights in a detention facility, then investigating crimes as a Texas State Enforcement Agent. After observing the underbelly of society, her fantasy stories allow her and her readers to escape into imagined worlds and inspire bravery in children (and adults alike) to face some of life's evil characters.

www.ingramcontent.com/pod-product-compliance
Lightning Source LLC
Chambersburg PA
CBHW011434240626
47153CB00011B/2993